The Betrayed

The Betrayed

KIERA CASS

HARPER TEEN
An Imprint of HarperCollinsPublishers

HarperTeen is an imprint of HarperCollins Publishers.

The Betrayed
Copyright © 2021 by Kiera Cass
Map by Virginia Allyn
All rights reserved. Printed in the United States of America.
No part of this book may be used or reproduced in any manner whatsoever
without written permission except in the case of
brief quotations embodied in critical articles and reviews.
For information address HarperCollins Children's Books, a division of
HarperCollins Publishers, 195 Broadway, New York, NY 10007.
www.epicreads.com
Library of Congress Control Number: 2021932074
ISBN 978-0-06-229166-0 (trade) — ISBN 978-0-06-311771-6 (special edition)
ISBN 978-0-06-308598-5 (int.)
Typography by Sarah Hoy and Erin Fitzsimmons
21 22 23 24 25   PC/LSCH   10 9 8 7 6 5 4 3 2 1
❖
First Edition

For Tara, who has been listening to my young adult stories since we were actual young adults. My Sunshine, there are too many inside jokes to insert, so just write your favorite one in the space below:

....

....

Ha ha! Oh my goodness, same!

From the

CHRONICLES OF COROAN HISTORY,

BOOK I

And so, Coroans, preserve the law,

For if we undo one, we undo them all.

ONE

As THE CARRIAGE ROLLED ON, I looked over my shoulder out the tiny rear window, as if someone might be coming after me. I reminded myself the notion was ridiculous; there wasn't anyone left in Coroa to follow me. Not anymore.

Silas—my husband—was dead, as were my parents. I still had a few friends at court, but they were far more loyal to King Jameson, and that would be especially true in the wake of me jilting him the very night he planned to propose. As for Jameson himself . . . at least it seemed I had his forgiveness for running away with a commoner—a foreign commoner, no less. Even so, Delia Grace had taken my place by the king's side, and I didn't want it back.

That was everyone. The only other people I cared about were in the carriage beside me. Still, I looked.

"I spent the majority of my adult life doing the exact same thing," my mother-in-law, Lady Eastoffe, commented, placing a hand on my lap. Across from us, my sister-in-law, Scarlet, slept on the other bench. Even in sleep, there was something about her posture that said she was ready to wake in a split second, a demeanor she'd adopted since the attack.

Just out the side window, Etan, proud and irritating on his horse, kept watch. He surveyed the thin mist, and I could tell by the way he kept tilting his head that he was listening for signs of danger.

"Hopefully after this trip, we can all stop looking behind us," I commented.

Lady Eastoffe—no, she was my mother now—nodded, looking solemnly at Scarlet. "Hopefully, once we reach the Northcotts, we'll find a way to confront King Quinten. After that, everything will be settled . . . one way or another."

I swallowed, reflecting on the finality of those words. One day, we would either walk out of King Quinten's palace victorious, or we'd never walk out.

Studying my new mother, it was still shocking to know she'd willingly walked into a marriage that tied her so closely to such a wicked king. But, then again, I'd unwittingly done the same.

The Eastoffes were descendants of Jedreck the Great, the first in the long-running line of kings on the Isolten throne. Isolte's current ruler, King Quinten, was descended from the first *son* of Jedreck, but not his first *child*. The East-offes were descendants of Jedreck's third son. Only dear old

Etan—a Northcott—could boast a lineage dating back to Jedreck's firstborn child, a daughter who had been passed over in favor of a boy.

Whatever the history, Quinten saw all Eastoffes and Northcotts as threats to his reign, which was coming to a swift close unless his son suddenly took a turn to better health.

I didn't understand it.

I didn't understand why he seemed intent on driving away—no, *murdering*—men who held royal blood. Prince Hadrian was not exactly the stoutest of souls, and when King Quinten himself died, as all mortals do, *someone* would have to take the throne. It made no sense to me that he was killing off everyone with a legitimate claim to it.

Silas included.

So, here we were, determined to ensure that the ones we lost didn't die in vain and painfully aware of how likely we were to fail in the process.

"Who goes there?" We heard the barking call over the squeaking of the wheels. Instantly, the carriage pulled to a stop. Scarlet was immediately upright, her hand pulling out of her skirts a small knife I didn't know she'd been hiding.

"Soldiers," Etan murmured. "Isolten." Then louder, he called: "Good afternoon. I am Etan Northcott, a soldier in His Majesty's—"

"Northcott? That you?"

I watched as Etan's face softened, his eyes squinting. He was suddenly much more at ease.

"Colvin?" he called back. There was no answer, so I took it to the affirmative. "I'm escorting my family back home from Coroa. By now you will have heard about my uncle. I'm bringing his widow and daughters home."

There was a pause, hinting at the confusion this created, when the soldier started speaking again.

"Widow? Surely you don't mean Lord Eastoffe is dead?"

Etan's horse bucked beneath him, but he steadied him quickly. "Indeed. And his sons. I was charged by my father to bring the rest of the family back to safety."

There was an uncomfortable silence.

"Our condolences to your family. We will let you through, but we must do a security check. Protocol."

"Yes, of course," Etan agreed. "I understand."

The soldier approached to examine our carriage while another walked around the outside, looking beneath the frame. By his voice, I recognized that the one looking in on us was the one Etan had been speaking with. "My Lady Eastoffe," he said, tipping his head toward Mother. "I'm so sorry for your loss."

"We thank you for your concern. And for your service," she replied.

"You ladies are lucky to have been met by the best regiment in Isolte," he said, puffing his chest. "This road is usually crawling with Coroans. They set fire to a border village not two weeks ago. If they'd come upon you, I don't know what would have happened."

I swallowed, looking down, then turned my eyes back

to the soldier. The connection of an additional lady in the Eastoffe family and the direction we were coming from all came together for him in an instant. He squinted at me and then looked back to Etan for confirmation.

"My cousin Silas's widow," he explained.

The soldier shook his head. "Can't believe Silas is gone . . . or that he married," he added, looking back at me. In his head, he seemed to be amending his thoughts, tacking on that what he really couldn't believe was that he'd married a Coroan.

Not many people could.

His eyes shifted from slightly judgmental to entertained. "Can't blame you for wanting to get out of there," he said to me, lifting his chin to the road behind us. "I don't keep up with much going on in Coroa, but it's impossible not to hear how your king has all but gone mad."

"Really?" Etan asked. "It's not as if he was that sane in the first place."

The soldier laughed. "Agreed. But apparently some girl rejected him, and he's been erratic ever since. Rumors are he's taken an axe to one of his best boats, right there on the river where anyone could see. We've heard that he's got someone new but isn't faithful to her in any sense of the word. Heard he set his castle on fire a few weeks ago, too."

"I've been to Keresken," Etan said flatly. "A fire could only improve it."

It took everything in me to bite my tongue. Not even at his worst would Jameson want to destroy the pinnacle of

Coroan craftsmanship that was Keresken Castle.

The only rumor that might pain me if true was the thought of Jameson seeing other girls behind Delia Grace's back. I hated the idea of her thinking she'd finally gotten what she wanted and being so very wrong.

The soldier barked a laugh at Etan's quick wit, then became serious. "With how unpredictable he's been, there's talk of a possible invasion. That's why we have to check the carriages, even with those we trust. Seems Crazy King Jameson could do anything at this point."

I could feel myself blushing and hated it. None of this was true, of course. Jameson wasn't crazy or planning an invasion or anything of the sort . . . but the look of suspicion on that man's face told me to keep my thoughts to myself.

Mother placed a comforting hand on my knee and spoke out the window to the guard. "Well, we certainly under-stand and thank you again for your thoroughness. And I will make sure to say special prayers for all of you once we're safely home."

"It's clear," the other soldier called from the opposite side of the carriage.

"Of course it is," he replied loudly. "It's the Eastoffes, you nit." He shook his head, then backed away from the carriage. "Move the barricades!" he called to the others. "Let them through. Stay safe out there, Northcott."

Etan nodded to him, keeping his thoughts to himself for once.

As we came upon the border, I could see dozens of men

outside the window. Some saluted, showing their respect, while others simply gawked. I feared that maybe one of them would connect me to the girl who had allegedly driven her king to madness, that they'd demand that I get out of the carriage and go back to him.

No one did.

I'd walked into this journey willingly. More than that, I'd chased it down. But that one incident made me aware that I wasn't just crossing a border; I was stepping into a different world.

"It should be smooth sailing to the manor," Etan said when we were clear of the crowd.

Scarlet placed the knife that she'd kept tucked under her demure little hands beneath the folds of her skirts again. I shook my head; what exactly had she planned to do with that anyway? Mother reached over and wrapped an arm around me. "One obstacle down, countless more to go," she joked.

And, for what it was worth, I laughed.

TWO

It took the better part of the day moving at a much faster pace than we had previously taken to make it to the Northcotts' manor. I knew we were getting close when Scarlet started paying attention to things outside the carriage and almost smiling, as if the area brought back happy memories.

The transformation of the climate and terrain happened quickly, as if acting by some unseen trigger. There were many rolling fields, the wind making the tall grass dance before us. We passed several rows of windmills that were taking advantage of the never-ending source of power that blew across the roads and up into the carriage. And then there were interesting little pockets of forests, with trees growing in small patches, as if they were huddling together in one place to keep warm.

Finally, the driver turned, leading the carriage between two rows of tall trees that lined a drive and led up to the front of a manor. Spotlights of sun filtered through the branches, making even the plainest objects sparkle. The way the stones that lined the drive had been worn round, the way the ivy climbed to the very top of the sides of the house, told me what I already knew: this family had been here forever.

Mother had been lost in thought the majority of the ride, but she finally let a glimmer of a smile reach her lips. As we neared the house, she poked her head out of the side window in the most unladylike fashion, waving with a fresh level of enthusiasm.

"Jovana!" she called, bounding down from the carriage as soon as we had come to a stop.

"Oh, Whitley, I've been so worried! How was the trip? Were the roads bad? Scarlet! I'm so happy to see you!" Jovana gushed upon seeing her niece, not waiting for answers to her questions.

"We have an unexpected guest," Etan informed his parents, his tone communicating his continued disapproval.

Raised to be a gentleman, he still lifted up a hand to help me out of the carriage. Raised to be a lady, I took it.

"Lady Hollis?" Lord Northcott asked, surprised.

"Oh, Lady Hollis! You poor thing!" Lady Northcott rushed to embrace me. "I can't believe you came all this way. Did you have nowhere else to go?"

"She's the mistress of her own estate now," Etan shared.

"She has a very comfortable manor; I've seen it myself."

"But it's lacking a family," I added quietly. "I had to be with my family."

"How brave," Lady Northcott commented, running her hand down my cheek. "Of course you are always welcome at Pearfield. Now, what you need is some rest. You are most welcome—and safe—here."

Etan rolled his eyes, spilling the truth with a single motion: we weren't really safe anywhere.

Lord Northcott walked over and took Scarlet's hand. "We've prepared the room overlooking the forest for you. And Lady Hollis, you—"

"Just Hollis. Please."

He smiled. "Certainly. We'll have fresh linens brought into the room right across the hall. Such a wonderful surprise."

Etan huffed.

His mother elbowed him.

I just let it all go.

"Let's get you settled in," Lady Northcott insisted. "I'm sure it's been quite the journey."

We were led upstairs to a branch of the house with four rooms, two on either side of the hallway. Mother was taken to another wing, presumably to have some peace, while Scarlet and I were left with Etan, whose renewed frustration was instantly clearer. Not only was I staying under his roof, I was in the room beside his. He glared at me before walking into it and shutting his door with so much force I felt it in my bones.

My room overlooked the front of the estate, showing the sweeping plains that welcomed guests to the Northcotts' home. There was no denying it made an impressive statement. If I wasn't so obviously out of place, it could almost remind me of home.

I peeked back into Scarlet's room and saw that she had gotten a view of the back stretch of the property. Most interesting to me was the line of dense trees to the one side that had an unmistakable gap where a well-worn path carved its way to the back of the house from the forest.

I left the door to my room open so I could listen to Scarlet across the hall. Her door was open as well, and I could hear her putting things away and moving furniture.

Scarlet had her own sounds. I knew her footsteps and breaths as I knew no one else's. Perhaps I could pick Delia Grace's determined march out of a crowd of others, but it was nothing like how I knew Scarlet now. Maybe it was a few weeks of sharing a bed, but she was a kind of home for me, a safe place. If I hadn't thought that she needed some space for herself right now, I'd have asked to stay with her.

Lady Northcott appeared in my doorway, a pile of gowns in her hand. "I hope I'm not disturbing you," she said, holding up the dresses. "I couldn't help but notice you didn't bring much in the way of clothes. I thought maybe we could recut some of these. I fear that eventually we'll have to go to court, and I thought it might make you more comfortable if you had . . . not that there's anything wrong with your clothes! It's just . . . oh dear."

I walked over, placing a hand on her shoulder. "This is very thoughtful. Thank you. I happen to be handy with a needle, and it will do me good to have something to focus on."

She let out a sigh that spoke of a lifetime of sadness. "We've lost so many over the years, and I still never know what to say to those left behind."

I shook my head. "I've never gone through anything like this. . . . Does it get any easier?"

She pressed her lips together in a tight, sad smile. "I wish I could tell you yes." She rebalanced the dresses in her hands. "There's good light in the drawing room. Do you want to come with me?"

I nodded.

"Very good. Let me just go get Scarlet and Etan. It's been too long since we've all been in the same room."

Annoyed, I followed her into the hallway.

The air in the room was unmistakably tense. Etan was on the prowl, scowling and shooting glances at the door like he was waiting for an appropriate time to run. Scarlet, too, was clearly counting the moments until she could escape, and Mother was speaking to Lord Northcott in hushed tones, making plans they weren't quite ready to share.

"Those two have always been plotters," Lady Northcott said, noting my stare.

"Plotters? What are they working on?" I kept looking between her and them. She was struggling to get a thread into the eye of the needle, and I watched as she adorably stuck her tongue out a bit as she focused. "Here," I offered. "I'll thread, you can pin."

I glanced up to see Etan walking behind her, glowering as he watched us. My hands weren't nearly as steady when he looked at me like that. His eyes landed on the ring on my right hand, the one that Mother had given me. It had belonged to Jedreck, and it had been passed down through the Eastoffe family over the generations.

He didn't think I should have it, and, for that matter, neither did I. But I wore it with love. Receiving that ring had saved her life and mine.

"Thank you, dear girl. Oh, they're working on the same thing they're always working on. They—"

"Mother . . ." Etan looked between her and me hesitantly. "Are you sure you should be telling her this?"

She sighed. "My darling boy, she's in the thick of it now. I don't think we can keep her in the dark."

Unsatisfied, he straightened his back and continued circling the room like a vulture.

"Since the beginning of his reign, something has been . . . off about Quinten, though the outright attacks on Isoltens who dare to oppose him only started happening in the last decade or so. He oughtn't be king, and our family is searching for the right way to go about removing him."

I squinted as I pulled the thread taut. "If a king is truly awful, isn't there usually a revolt? Don't people just get angry and take the castle?"

She sighed. "One would think. But, as a Coroan, I know

you understand when I say that Isolte is a land of laws. Quinten's disposition leads us to believe he's pulling the strings behind every awful thing that's ever happened in Isolte, and he's certainly never done anything to contradict the notion. But . . . what if we're wrong? What if it's some lone vigilante? What if it's Hadrian, who has no means of physically protecting himself, using others to knock opponents down? What if it's some group of rogues acting on their volition? Attempting to overthrow a king without just cause is against the law, but the act of doing so *with* just cause is lawful. If we could only catch him in action, we would have the proof we need. We would have the support of thousands of years of edicts and commandments behind us and, once we spread the truth widely, the support of the people at large. Without that, we'd be seen as lawless usurpers. . . . Anything we attempted would be unmade as quickly as we built it."

"So, that's the problem? No one's ever seen him with their own eyes making an order or drawing a sword?" I asked.

Etan's footsteps clearly fell behind me, then became quieter as he walked down the length of the room. I took a breath, feeling much calmer without him over my shoulder.

She nodded. "And if anyone could figure out a way to do it, it's those two. Sharpest minds of us all when it comes to plans."

"Well then, at least we're in good hands. I'm just happy nothing like that is up to me! I don't have that kind of talent."

She smiled. "You have talents all your own, Hollis. I've

seen them in action. And that's what matters. We all must use everything we have to make a difference."

"Indeed." I looked across the room at Etan. Silas had sworn Etan was talented himself. I knew him to be a soldier, and he seemed calm under pressure. He lacked many other admirable qualities—kindness being at the top of the list—but I couldn't deny he had a quick mind. That didn't make me admire him, though.

He downed the last of his drink and set his cup down so loud it rang throughout the room, drawing my attention whether I wanted to give it to him or not. His eyes studied me. There was something about his glare that chilled me through and through. In a single look Etan Northcott made it shockingly clear that he hated me—and was desperate to see me gone.

But he was not the head of this household, and it seemed, as far as his parents were concerned, I was more than welcome. As if reading my thoughts and wanting to show just how much a part of this I was, Lord Northcott stood and walked our way.

"Is my wife informing you of what an ordeal you've walked into? Of all the plans you're now tied up in?" he asked. His movement prompted his son, who was now back to circling.

I smiled up at him. "I had an idea. But I didn't realize how much work you've been doing here, trying to make things right. On that front, it seems I have much to learn."

He sat down in a large chair across from me as Mother came to stand, her hands resting on the back of said chair.

"I cannot think of a better time to tell you what we know, what we've guessed, and what we're working on."

"Are you sure that's wise?" Etan whispered, though it wasn't as if I wouldn't hear. Twice now he'd publicly expressed I was not to be trusted.

Lord Northcott smiled at his son, not judging him, not even really correcting him, but simply stating the obvious in his eyes. "Yes, I think my new niece should be included in our plans, shaky as they are."

Etan's eyes went to me again, and I could see that air of suspicion in them.

"Lady Northcott already started explaining some of this," I offered. "It sounds like what we need is proof that King Quinten is behind the Darkest Knights' actions before he can be overthrown?"

"Essentially. So, for now, finding proof is our strategy." Lord Northcott sighed. "Not that we haven't attempted before, of course," he said, speaking mainly to me. "We've tried to bribe guards. We have friends who live at court with eyes always open. We have . . . well, more support than one might guess. But, so far, we haven't had much success." He met all of our eyes in turn. "And with how violent and frequent the attacks have been, I feel that whatever it is we do next might be our last attempt at revealing Quinten's actions. All of us are to work on this. What do we know already? Who might be able to aid us in this? Which reminds me. Etan?" He turned away to face his son. "Did you hear anything as you passed into or out of Coroa? I assumed your fellow soldiers would speak without their guards up around you."

He nodded slowly, unwilling to speak right away. "I did. It seems the queen has lost her child and is trying for another."

I looked at him, hating to be so desperate for news that only he could give.

"How is Valentina?"

He squinted at me and shrugged. "I don't typically ask about the welfare of my enemies."

It was a word I was certain he associated with me as well.

"She's just a young woman," I countered. "She's done nothing."

"She's the *wife* of my enemy. She's trying to add to the most ruthless royal family in the history of the line. She certainly isn't a friend."

"She's *my* friend," I whispered.

He didn't bother replying, moving on with his news.

"Quinten is trying to perpetuate the idea that she's with child, but the women of court say she has no cravings and is still active, so I can't say there's much to it."

I swallowed, imagining Valentina alone in her castle, probably both thankful that she'd been given another chance and terrified of what was coming for her if she failed. I couldn't see that pressure helping with the process.

"Prince Hadrian was ill of late. Well, more so than usual. He missed a few days at court, and when he was brought back out, he could hardly walk. I don't know what King Quinten thinks he's accomplishing there, parading Hadrian around when he's so weak."

"Poor boy," Lady Northcott sighed. "I don't know how he's managed to stay alive as long as he has. It will be a miracle if he lives to see his wedding day."

"When is that to come again?" Mother asked.

"She's supposed to arrive early next year," Lady Northcott confirmed.

"I'm still shocked they went abroad to find a bride for him," Lord Northcott commented.

"Is it so extraordinary that Prince Hadrian would marry another royal?" I asked.

"Yes," the others replied almost simultaneously.

I raised my eyebrows at that. "Huh. Before I left, I was unofficially placed on a contract. My firstborn daughter—assuming she had an older brother to inherit the throne—was to marry Hadrian's eldest son. Jameson said it was uncharacteristic of King Quinten to arrange such a thing, for any Isolten royal to marry outside the country. I guess he was right."

Lord Northcott stared at me. "Is that true?"

I darted my eyes around the room and saw that everyone was leaning in, watching me in surprise.

"Yes. Jameson and Quinten signed the contract, but Hadrian, Valentina, and I were in the room. I suppose nothing will come of it now, since I wasn't properly named on it. Or perhaps the weight of it will transfer to Delia Grace. Why? What is it?"

"What could that be about?" Lord Northcott wondered aloud.

"Legitimacy," Etan said quickly. "They want other royal

blood in the line so that no one can question their descendants' claim to the throne. In return, he's offering Coroans the allegiance of Isolte, the largest kingdom on the continent." Etan shook his head. "It's brilliant."

There was a long silence as everyone took this in. King Quinten was making plans to protect himself and his line, and we were still sitting here with no idea of how to even attack.

"Is there anything we can do about this?" I asked quietly.

Lord Northcott's brow was knit tight as he drummed his fingers against each other. "I don't think so, but that's good information to have. Thank you, Hollis. Is there anything else you can think of, anything from that trip in particular, that you think might be of value?"

I swallowed. "I hate to disappoint, but I was strongly encouraged to keep my distance from Quinten when he was visiting, so we only spoke briefly."

The one, quick interaction shot through my memory, and it was as painfully clear as a punch to the chest.

"Oh." I felt my body go cold. It seemed too much of a coincidence to actually be one.

"What?" Etan asked. "Does he have other plans?"

I shook my head, my eyes brimming with tears against my will. "He warned me."

"Who? Quinten?" Mother asked.

I nodded. I could feel the tears spilling over as I flashed back into the Great Hall of Keresken Castle. I was holding the crown Silas had made. He'd been standing right beside me when it happened. "He noticed I'd gotten close to your family . . . and he . . . I can't remember the exact words, but he told me to be careful, or I'd get burned."

Mother covered her mouth with her hand, her face a mask of horror.

He knew. He knew even then he was going to kill them, and he could guess I was going to be close enough to the Eastoffes that I would be in danger myself.

"Father, is that not enough?" Etan asked.

"I'm afraid not, my son. It is a brick, but we need a wall."

I sat there, still stunned by Quinten's words, and trying to think of anything else he might have said.

"Are you all right, Hollis?" Scarlet asked quietly. She'd been so quiet, I'd almost forgotten she was there. But she understood. She was haunted in her own way.

I nodded, though it was a lie. Sometimes it felt like Silas had been dead for years, one chapter in a book that I'd finished reading long ago. But other times, it felt like the pain of losing him was so new it ripped the wound open and forced it wider, leaving my very heart bleeding over a love so young it had barely learned to walk.

I dabbed at my tears. I could cry when I was alone. Not here.

"Speaking of the attack, there is another detail that concerns me."

I looked over at Etan, watching as he toyed with his cuffs, looking as if he simply needed something to occupy his hands.

"And what is that?" Mother inquired.

"News of it hadn't reached the lines at all."

"So?" Mother asked.

"That the king succeeded in nearly cutting down an entire branch of the family seems like something everyone would know about. If not from his own gloating, from others' fear. But they said nothing of it when I traveled to Coroa, and they knew nothing when we passed back into Isolte today." He shook his head. "I think we need to be on guard."

Lord Northcott looked up at him, serious and calm. "We are always on guard."

"Yes, but this event is startling," Etan insisted, gesturing to Mother. "By now, the rumors ought to be swelling. They're not. If the king is silencing people, we very well might be his next target."

"You're letting your imagination run away with you, son. We have always been wary where the king is concerned, but there's no reason for us to run around in a panic. We are still descendants of a princess, not a prince. Queen Valentina is still young, and Prince Hadrian still lives. I think, in the near future, his focus will be on them, not us. For now, we will continue with a search for undeniable evidence. We will not hide, and we will not run."

Etan huffed but said no more, at least seeming to respect his father enough to obey. As far as I'd seen, he had little respect for much else.

But there was a part of me that completely understood Etan's concern. If the Darkest Knights would cavalierly dispose of bodies in front of King Quinten's palace to brag of their works, why was no one speaking of this?

There were too many questions floating around our situation, and none of us knew how we were going to find the answers.

THREE

It was midnight, and I still couldn't sleep. One thing I missed about Keresken Castle—which had irritated me so much toward the end—was the constant stream of sound. The whisper of maids, the scuttling of feet, and even the rattle of carriages in the distance became a lullaby for me, and in the weeks since I'd left, I hadn't grown used to its absence. I found myself straining my ears, hoping I'd find something to be the melody of an otherwise silent night. It didn't happen.

Sometimes, when the world was too quiet, other sounds came to my head, ones that I'd invented. I would hear Silas screaming. I would hear him pleading. Or sometimes my mother would be crying out instead. My mind tried to fill in the spaces of what it didn't know, imagining the worst. I tried to force myself to assume the best. I told myself my mother fainted from the fear of it all, and my father, distressed, was knelt over, clutching her hand. That way, he never saw death when it came, and she never felt it.

As for Silas, I couldn't imagine him not staring down anything that came at him, good or bad. If he screamed, it wouldn't have been for mercy or in fear. It would have been as he went down, fighting with every breath.

I tossed in my bed. I'd known my mind would be searching for other clues from King Quinten's visit to the palace, but there was nothing else to find. At least, it seemed like there wasn't. That didn't stop me from trying and then wishing for sleep and then realizing there were too many things in my mind fighting it, including the fact that someone who hated me was right next door.

I finally got out of bed, daring to venture across the hall to Scarlet's room. She wasn't sleeping well these days, either.

"Who's there?" she asked, sitting bolt upright in the moonlight at the sound of the creaking door. I had no doubt her knife was already in her hand.

"Just me."

"Oh. Sorry."

"No, I can't blame you. I'm not feeling exactly at ease myself right now." I climbed into the bed beside her. It was familiar. When I'd first left court and was being sheltered by the Eastoffes, it was Scarlet's room I shared. Those were comfortable days—us crammed into a bed that needed about as much repair as the rest of the house, waking up with someone's slow and sleepy breathing to let us know we weren't alone.

We'd sing songs in whispers and laugh at old stories and rumors of court. I'd been an only child my whole life. Being swallowed into a family with older siblings and younger siblings and, most important, a sister was a dream come true.

The mood was decidedly different now.

"I keep thinking about Quinten's visit to Keresken and trying to remember anything he might have said or done that we could use as proof . . . nothing's coming to mind, and it's pushing me to madness."

"Ah, well, you'll fit in here perfectly," she said as I settled under the blankets. "We probably should have asked to share a room. After living in that tiny space in the castle, I realized how much I liked having my family nearby. It was a treat that we needed to share back at Abicrest."

"I had the same thought. I just didn't want to be rude. Your aunt and uncle have been so generous."

"They really like you," she said. "Aunt Jovana keeps saying you have an uplifting presence."

I chuckled humorlessly. "My parents had other words for that, but I'm glad she appreciates me all the same. If only Etan would stop glaring at me."

"Just ignore him for now."

"I'm trying, I swear." I sighed and gave the one real question I had a voice. "Do we have a chance here, Scarlet? You've been in this since birth, so you'd know better than I would."

She swallowed. "Our support runs deep. For years we've all but had an army ready to go. I know Aunt Jovana told you about the law . . ."

"She did. I can't say I don't understand, but these seem like extenuating circumstances."

She replied, her tone low and serious, "If we were wrong, it would mean death for everyone involved. And if we didn't act fast enough, the Darkest Knights could come and wipe us all out before we even began. I want to see him pay . . . but we have to do it right or it's all for nothing."

I sighed again. In my eyes, it was hard to imagine that there was a right way to fix so much wrong, but if this was what the family said to do, then I'd follow.

"Do you know why we left Isolte?" Scarlet asked.

"Silas told me it was his idea, and Mother said your livestock was slaughtered . . . I'd have left, too."

She shook her head. "Remember—if we remove Quinten from the throne, he has to be replaced with *somebody* . . . someone with Jedreck's royal blood."

I sat up, tracing the obvious line of events in my head, unable to believe I'd never considered it before now.

"Silas?"

She nodded. "Firstborn son of the male line . . . he was the one people talked about. Well, the ones who were daring enough to speak at all."

I hung my head, thinking of how selfish I'd been. An entire country lost something when Silas Eastoffe died. I wondered if what Etan said was true, if people didn't know he was gone yet. I wondered if they'd started pinning their hopes on . . .

"Scarlet," I gasped. "Are you saying . . . *you* could be queen?"

She sighed, toying with the blanket. "I've been praying it doesn't come to that. Part of why we came back was to throw our support behind Uncle Reid. He should be king."

"But . . . but you could *rule*. You could shape the world around you any way you want."

"You had that option, once. By the looks of that letter Jameson sent before we left, it was very nearly offered to you again. Would you go back to that if you could?"

"No," I answered quickly. "But I wasn't going to be sovereign. You would."

She shrugged. "People might back me, but it's certainly not a given, the way it was with Silas."

A shiver ran through me. "So he knew, then? That people supported him?"

She swallowed. "We started making a plan once, maybe four months before we came to Coroa. If you can imagine, Mother and Uncle Reid were plotting even more than they are now. Even though we didn't have the proof we needed, we thought we could make the move because of the people. They're ready . . . but they're also terrified. But then all these rumors about Silas planning to storm the palace got out ahead of us. We couldn't stop it once it started. He wasn't ready, none of us were. There was talk at court, warning glances . . . we had a sense that, even though nothing had happened, the rumors alone had doomed Silas. So he begged Mother and Father to run, to save the family. They hoped we'd come back someday, and I think Silas would have loved to see Quinten brought to justice, but he wanted what we all wanted: a chance at life. He swore he'd never return. And then he met you. He had every reason to stay in Coroa."

I wasn't sure when I'd started crying, but I could taste the tears now. "And it didn't matter," I said. "He lost his life anyway. Quinten wasn't content to let him leave."

"No," she answered. "He takes and takes and takes. Maybe it should make us stop. But for me, it just makes me want to make him pay."

I was shaking as I lay back down. I kept thinking of Silas, so confident and funny and clever. I thought of him embracing me even though so many of his countrymen detested mine. I thought of him trying to make peace in whatever way he could.

He would have been a marvelous king.

But he didn't want that. He wanted other titles. Husband. Father. Friend. And he was denied all of those at Quinten's threatened hand.

"How do we make this right, Scarlet? How do we make him pay?"

"There's only one way I can think of to make sure it never happens again," she said plainly.

"Murder him?" I asked, hating to even think it. I didn't think the answer to death was more death.

"And Hadrian. And probably Valentina for good measure.

We'd have to remove the entire family."

I could hardly breathe thinking about it. "I couldn't lift a hand to Valentina. I still consider her a friend."

Scarlet stared at the ceiling, looking as if she was carefully thinking over her words. "I'm not sure there's a way to uncouple her from the royal family. She's the queen."

"I . . . Scarlet, I can't."

After a pause, she rolled to face me. "Can I ask you something completely unrelated to the topic?" she ventured.

"Yes, please."

"Do you think you'll ever remarry?"

I lifted my hand up and touched my chest. The ring Mother had given me was still proudly on my right hand, a sign of allegiance to my new family, but my rings from Silas were on a chain, and I kept them near my heart. These were the only pieces of jewelry I cared about anymore.

Sometimes I wondered if I should have kept my father's ring, the one that was handed down through the lines of old Coroan aristocracy. Seeing as I wasn't sure which of the charred rings we'd found in the remnants of the fire had been his, it probably never would have felt right.

"I don't know. Silas left a mark. I don't know if I want someone else to. No matter how much time passes, I don't think I'll ever forget what he did to me, for me. It probably doesn't seem like it right now, but I'll always feel like he rescued me."

She was quiet for a while. "I think he'd be happy to know that's how you felt, even after everything that's happened. I think he'd be happy to know you don't want to hurt anyone, too. He was like that."

I smiled. "I know." I still had a lifetime's worth of things to learn about Silas, but I knew his character, and I would carry that with me. I swallowed, unsure if I could speak about him more just now. "What about you? Do you want to get married?"

"I don't know if I can. Not anymore," she confessed. "I feel like there might always be a wall around me."

"That's a good way to put it. It's hard to think of letting anyone as close as I let Silas. . . . Before we left, I went by his grave. I told him I felt like I was going to have to let him go in a way so I could keep living."

"That's sort of how it works," Scarlet said plainly.

I looked over at her. "How many people have you lost?"

"Enough that I have learned I must let them be a landmark, not an anchor."

I reached out and grabbed her hand. "Please don't leave me, Scarlet."

"I have no plans to. I intend to be still standing at the end of this. Free."

"Good. I want to see that."

I was suddenly quite exhausted. Tired of hiding, tired of running, tired of trying to be so many things. I reached over, leaving my hand where Scarlet could hold it if she wanted to. She carefully laced her fingers through mine, and I finally felt safe enough to sleep.

In the morning, I woke to the sound of songbirds and

realized Scarlet and I were lying back to back, the warmth of another person taking away the bite of the cold air of sunrise. It was the most content I'd been in ages, and I had no desire to leave my bed.

As if reading my thoughts, Scarlet mumbled, "We have to go and eat now, don't we?"

"I brought some of my money from Jameson," I offered. "We could steal horses and become gypsies."

"I could pretend to read tea leaves and tell fortunes."

"If I can do an almain, surely I could learn to dance like they do."

"Absolutely," she affirmed. "You're a very gifted dancer."

"So are you. We'd really be quite the spectacle."

"We would." She paused. "But aren't there laws against travelers?"

"Probably. . . . So, then, it's prison or breakfast."

She sighed. "Do you think they feed you well in prison?"

I considered this. "Well, if it's between breakfast with Etan and prison, I'll take whatever they're serving."

FOUR

As I bent my arms in funny positions to lace up my dress, I remembered a season when it was a privilege to help me into my clothes. I did the best I could, but I was going to need Scarlet to finish doing up my sleeves.

I'd spent so many years waking up at Keresken Castle, but then I'd adjusted to waking up at Abicrest. And then, when it was gone, I got used to waking up at Varinger Hall. And today, here I was at Pearfield, waking up in yet another new place with new rules and rhythms. Before anything had even begun, I felt out of step.

I walked out of my room, hoping Scarlet would be waiting. She wasn't there yet, so I paced our very short corridor, letting my gaze wander around the hallway. I didn't want to critique the architecture, but it felt very plain. Sturdy, but plain. Why not carve into the support beams? Why not paint designs on the walls? There was so much space.

I tried to rein in my critical thoughts. Maybe there was something beautiful about the potential being left there, like the endless temptation of a blank page.

Ruining my quiet thoughts, Etan walked out of his room, adjusting his cuffs. He stopped dead in his tracks when he saw me, eyes narrowing as he looked me over. They were so cold, those eyes, a gray-blue color that reminded me of the sky when a storm was coming. And his stubble was growing out, making him look a little messy or crazy or angry . . . I couldn't find the word, but it wasn't positive.

"Your sleeves are untied," he commented.

"I know. I need another pair of hands, and I don't have a maid."

He crossed his arms. "You could send for one."

I wasn't sure I should mention that I'd sent for water yesterday to clean off, and it never showed. And, after no one came to prepare my room for the night, I'd built my own fire before bed. Very poorly, but still. "I did earlier, but so far, no one has come."

"Can't blame them. You certainly couldn't pay me enough." He walked closer, stopping in front of me. "What's your secret? I'll figure it out either way, but it would save us all some time if you told me now."

"I beg your pardon?"

"I know who you are, and I know how you were raised, and I know that your loyalty to Coroa is far deeper than it is to Isolte. So, why are you here? What's the real reason?"

I stared at him, shocked. "My parents are dead. My husband is dead. This is the only family I have. *That's* why I'm here."

He shook his head. "I saw the way Jameson Barclay looked at you. If you walked back into that castle, you'd be welcomed with open arms."

"His arms have been filled by another. I have no place in Jameson's court anymore."

He stood there, sizing me up. "I doubt that."

I lifted my hands in surrender. "I don't know what you're getting at, Etan. Silas was the last secret I had. So, whatever you think is happening here, you're wrong."

"I'm watching you," he warned.

"I've noticed," I countered.

Just then, Scarlet came from her room, and I saw her eyebrows rise at just how close he was to me. He glared at me in frustration and headed down the stairs as I held out my sleeves to Scarlet. She didn't need me to ask.

"What was that about?" she wondered, tying the tiny bows.

"Etan is watching me," I said. "I can't stand him."

She sighed. "Etan can be . . . passionate."

"Passionate? Is that the word you're going with?"

"But he can also be very kind, and even funny, once you get to know him."

I dropped my chin and scoffed. "Kind? Funny?"

"I know it doesn't seem like it now. We all deal with our pain in different ways. Etan lashes out. He just doesn't realize he's placing his efforts on the wrong target."

I considered this. "Am I just to wait until he figures that out?"

She nodded. "You're going to have to. He'll come around once he sees you like we do, and, quite frankly, you two are the least of my concerns right now."

The tension was getting to her, and I saw that her chest was rising and falling quickly, and that her hands were shaky as she tied the last bow. She wasn't here anymore; she was back in Abicrest, in the middle of the attack. "Do you want to talk about it?"

She shook her head. "Not yet."

"Well, if you ever decide you're ready . . ."

"I would tell you before anyone else. The others wouldn't understand, and Mother couldn't take it. Only not yet."

I took her hands, steadying them in my own. "That's fine. We'll make this right, Scarlet. Somehow, we'll figure this out."

She nodded, taking a few steadying breaths. She couldn't hide everything, but she wasn't prepared to show just how deeply this was hurting her, either. I felt privileged in a way, that she lowered her shields to me.

"I'm ready now," she said. "Let's go." We headed downstairs, arms laced. "I was thinking I might want to move to the country, in the north, far away from everything."

"I don't blame you. After the bustle of court life, something quiet might be nice. You know, once we overthrow a kingdom and dole out justice and all," I teased.

She smirked. "I'll find a house and keep a room especially for you, just in case you do get married and want somewhere to run when your husband is a pain."

I giggled and held her arm a little tighter. "Perhaps we'll just grow into old maids."

"With lots of goats," she suggested.

"I like goats."

"Then it's settled."

By the time we got to the dining room, Mother was already seated, as was Lord Northcott. They had been speaking in whispers, but looked up and smiled brightly when they saw us come in.

"Good morning, girls," Lord Northcott greeted us happily. "You look well rested."

"Then we have you fooled," Scarlet joked.

I'd expected Etan to already be there, but he must have had errands or something, because he walked into the room seconds after us.

He greeted his father and took the seat across from me, refusing to give me any space at all.

Pottage, cheeses, and bread were on the table. After Scarlet began spooning some onto her plate, I did the same. A maid poured some ale into Etan's and Scarlet's cups. I held mine up so I could get some as well. I couldn't tell if she didn't see me or ignored me.

I set my cup back down. Etan watched the whole thing unfold, and for some reason, him seeing me being snubbed was worse than the actual event itself, and I could feel myself blushing. I lowered my eyes and ate in silence.

"Ah! What a joy to see a full table!" Lady Northcott swung into the room, injecting the atmosphere with infectious bliss. I watched as she walked around the table to kiss her husband on his cheek and her son on his forehead. Etan didn't pull away or look irritated as he usually did but seemed to be thankful for the brief touch. I couldn't help but smile, aching a bit that my mother never did such a thing for me.

I wished we'd had more time.

"So, Hollis, I think you need a tour of the grounds today," she said, taking her seat and turning to me.

I sat up straighter. "I'd love one, Lady Northcott."

"Good. And I've been thinking," she started, picking up her spoon. "Hollis is part of the family now."

"Absolutely," Lord Northcott agreed. "Integral."

"So, we ought to drop the formalities. Hollis, can we simply be Aunt Jovana and Uncle Reid to you? As we are to Scarlet?"

All eyes fell on me, and I could see the hope in them. It was such a sweet and generous offer that, even if I'd felt a little uncomfortable, I couldn't say no.

"If it would please you," I eked out.

My new aunt Jovana smiled with such brilliance, but I couldn't appreciate it. All I could see was the look of disdain on the maid's face and the look of pure disappointment on Etan's. It wasn't his typical angry mask but something more painful. Like I'd infiltrated something that was his and claimed it as my own.

"We are so happy to have you, Hollis." She settled her napkin across her lap. "It's such a wonderful change. We're so used to losing people—my sweet nephews, my two girls—" I swallowed hard at her words, realizing now just where her sorrow stemmed from. "Finally, we've added someone!"

"Hear, hear," Mother agreed.

Uncle Reid was smiling, and even Scarlet looked peaceful. But I couldn't shake the coldness rolling off Etan in sharp and heavy waves. If I thought I'd crossed a line before, it was nothing compared to this.

FIVE

"THESE TREES WERE PLANTED BY the first Northcotts at Pearfield," Aunt Jovana claimed, pointing to the row of trees along the back of the property. "We're lucky to have such strong ones. They protect the house during the windiest seasons and allow for some natural privacy."

"I can't help but notice they missed a spot," I joked, pointing to the space in the line that had the path worn into it.

She laughed. "We took that one out ourselves about twenty years ago now. That path gives us easy access to those who work our land, which extends out from that line. You'll see the importance firsthand tomorrow; it's a bread day."

I didn't know what a bread day was, but I supposed I'd learn in the morning. Scarlet squeezed the hand she was holding, drawing my attention to her. She smiled, and I could see she was trying to soothe my nerves; Etan was a few steps behind us.

He certainly didn't need a tour of his own grounds, but it appeared I wasn't allowed to wander them without his watchful eye on me. Did he think I was going to take an axe to the manor or something? Lift a curtain and produce an army? I sighed, trying unsuccessfully to ignore him.

"And as we come around the side of the house, you'll have an excellent view of our garden. You see, we place large shrubs around the edges to help with the wind, and it allows the blossoming plants to fare better. They've all come in so nicely this year."

I looked longingly at the flowers. Oh, how I missed the garden at Kereken; it had been my hiding place.

"Perhaps we should go pick some? For the dinner table?" Aunt Jovana suggested, noting the desire in my eyes.

"Could we?"

"Of course!"

I looked up at her thick hair. "I have a better idea." I took her arm and pulled her into the heart of the garden, hunting for a bench. "All right, Scarlet. You find the prettiest blossoms and bring them to me."

"Aye, aye, captain," she joked, heading into the high walls of greenery. Etan planted himself by the edge of the garden, his back against a tall shrub. He crossed his arms, watching over everything intently.

I got Aunt Jovana to sit, and I started to pull the pins from her hair.

"What in the world are you doing?" she asked with a chuckle.

"Making a masterpiece," I assured her. "Now sit still."

I pulled up pieces of her hair, braiding it the way I used to braid Delia Grace's. I wondered who took care of her now. I wondered if she missed me at all, or if Nora did. The ache of losing my family and Silas had pushed my friends from my thoughts for so long, but now that they were there, I wished I could embrace them both, even if only for a moment.

Scarlet brought back flowers as blue as the Isolten flag, and I placed them in the crown of a braid I'd woven in Aunt Jovana's hair as she sat there laughing. After we'd filled up her hair, I put the flowers in Scarlet's and my own, and then I set some aside for Mother.

If we were going to fight, then we needed something to fight for. For the freedom of choosing our own dinner or riding as far as we dreamed. For the hope of tomorrow or flowers in our hair. The grand and the small; it all mattered.

I noted Etan's eyes weren't on me anymore; they were on his mother. And he seemed to have a hint of a smile on his face as he watched her, his arms still crossed, head tilted to the side.

I pulled a flower from the pile I'd set aside and walked over to him. When I was halfway to him, he noticed me, and his demeanor changed in an instant. Hesitant, on guard. I reached up and wordlessly looped a flower through a buttonhole on his chest. He scowled at it and then me with those slate-colored eyes. But he didn't rip it out, and he didn't make a comment.

I tipped my head and went back to the ladies, happy to make my way through the garden and around the rest of the Northcotts' lands.

I'd been standing in my nightgown with my door open for quite some time now. Isolte was cold at night, and I needed to start a fire. If the maids wouldn't light one, fine; I knew how to do it myself. But I'd used all the wood I had, and I didn't know where to get any more.

Finally, I crossed my arms and went over to Scarlet's room. I knocked, but no one answered. I risked a quick peek in, but she wasn't there. Her fire, I noted, was lit, but there were only two logs left over. I couldn't take that from her.

Closing the door, I moved to the empty room beside hers, hoping that perhaps it had been stocked in advance. Unfortunately, that was not the case. It seemed I'd only gotten my first cache of wood under the watchful eye of Aunt Jovana as she ordered an extra room to be prepared.

I'd ask her for some, but I didn't know where her rooms or Mother's were. I was stuck.

I sighed, looking across the hallway to Etan's door. And I asked myself if I would rather speak to him or potentially lose a few toes to frostbite. . . .

Shoving away my pride, I walked across the floor and knocked. I heard him springing up and was surprised when he opened the door so forcefully.

"What's wrong?" he asked urgently.

I was temporarily distracted by the fact that his shirt was both untucked and untied, half of it slung off his shoulder. I could see at least three different scars on his chest, presumably marks from his time as a soldier.

"Everyone is fine," I said, holding up a hand. "No emergency."

He let out a long breath and nodded, as if needing to calm himself down. In a split second he had jumped to the worst conclusion, and he had to undo all the anxiety he'd built up. It was a sensation I understood too well.

"It's just . . . ," I began, then hesitated.

"Spit it out."

"The maids won't bring me firewood, and I don't know where to find it myself. Could I please have some of yours?"

Ugh, I wished I could wipe the smug little smirk off his face. "So, the mighty Lady Hollis needs a favor."

"Don't do this, Etan." I tried to look brave in the midst of being humbled. "Imagine how cold I must be if I'm willing to ask you. Please, give me some of your firewood."

There was a long pause, and I waited for him to slam the door in my face.

"Come in," he finally said, and I followed him inside, holding my head high.

In my mind I'd imagined him to be messy, but his things were mostly tidy. He had three books open on a desk, and a few extra cups that looked used on the table by his bed, but he didn't have clothes strewn about the floor, and it didn't smell in here.

"Hold your arms out," he commanded, and I did as I was told. He started piling split logs across my hands, and I watched them, adjusting my grip so I'd hopefully avoid splinters. "The firewood is out back, stacked between two trees. You can get your own tomorrow."

"I will," I said.

"You owe me one. I ought to make you go get your own now."

I sighed, finally looking up. "Etan, I don't . . ."

My words were stolen by the sight of something so both foreign and familiar, it brought tears to my eyes.

On the wall, mounted just above Etan's fireplace, was a sword with a large V-shaped chip in the blade.

"What?" Etan demanded.

I said nothing, passing him to get closer to the sword.

"Where do you think you're going?" he demanded, trailing behind me.

I stopped in front of the fireplace, looking up at it. It was almost like I could feel Silas here.

"What are you doing?" he asked rather loudly. "Need I remind you, this is *my* room?"

"Do you know the first time I heard your name, Etan?" I asked in a whisper. "Silas was telling me about how he started working with metal, and he told me about a sword he made for his cousin. He said that even though he did a terrible job, you used it the entire tournament."

I managed to tear my eyes away long enough to look at him. His eyes were cautious as we both turned and stared up at the battered metal on the wall.

"It's all but unusable," he replied, his voice soft. "If I hit that chip again, it'll break, and the handle is so unreliable. But I can't get rid of it. Even before everything happened, I couldn't have parted with it. He was very proud."

I nodded. "I admired that, his pride." I kept my eyes up, staring at Silas's work, trying to breathe through the tightness in my chest. "My first impression of you, from that stolen conversation with a boy I was never supposed to know, was of someone with integrity, someone who was gracious." I looked over to him again. "You are unrecognizable in comparison to the person Silas told me about. Or even the person Scarlet tells me about. You're some stranger in that man's place. Why?"

There was a long breath of silence.

"Get out of my room."

"I really want to understand. What is it that makes you so cold when your family has told me you're not like that at all?"

"I said, get out." He pointed to the door, and after a moment, I obeyed. In the hallway, I turned back to look at him. His eyes were now both ice and fire. "Don't you think you've taken enough from me?" he asked. "Go home."

I shook my head. "I don't know how else to show you, Etan. I'm here for my family. And I won't leave them."

The slamming door I'd been expecting earlier finally came, and I hated that I wanted him to open the door again, just so I could look at Silas's terrible sword. I went back to my room and used my candle to start a fire.

I sat as close to it as I could, toying with my wedding ring on its chain and crying. And seeing as I could hear Etan huffing around his room in anger, I was sure he could hear me, too.

SIX

EARLY THE FOLLOWING MORNING, I learned what a bread day was. The Northcotts made huge batches of bread twice a week for the families who tended their land. It meant that all the cooks, some of the maids, and Aunt Jovana herself were in the kitchen shortly after sunrise, working and baking throughout the day. It ensured that, even if someone who worked for them was sick, they had something to eat. It was one of the most generous and simple ideas I'd ever heard of, and I was eager to participate.

If only eagerness could translate to skill.

Scarlet stayed close as we watched the cooks folding dough in on itself so aggressively, I wondered if it would leave the whole thing bruised. We tried to mirror their actions, but neither of us were as strong as the women who'd been doing this for ages. Even Aunt Jovana was impressive, lifting up the dough and slapping it on the table with force. I was too afraid it'd fly from my hand if I attempted anything close to that.

If I wasn't daunted enough by the mastery of the cooks around me, Etan's ever-watching eyes seeing me fail was making it a hundred times worse.

"Son, if you're going to be down here, why don't you help us?" Aunt Jovana asked, darting her eyes to where he sat, legs wide on a counter and taking spitefully loud bites of an apple.

"Nope. I'm here to be close to Enid, and that's all," he declared, a lock of his hair casually flipping across his forehead.

"None of that nonsense!" the large woman beside me exclaimed, but I could see she was amused by him flirting. Meanwhile, I was completely thrown by his behavior.

"You're the love of my life, Enid. I'd die without you!" he exclaimed, his mouth still full of apple.

The women in the room laughed. Clearly, I was in a room of Etan supporters. It baffled me. Was this who he was when I wasn't around? Was his natural state one of charm? And, in an entirely unrelated issue, why could I not figure out how to roll dough?

"Give me that," Enid said, pulling the dough from me. "If you don't work it right, the bread won't rise."

"Sorry," I mumbled. I peeked over my shoulder, and Etan was watching me, shaking his head. If it was so easy, then why wasn't he doing it?

"Enid here has been making bread since she was tall enough to reach the table. You can learn plenty from her," Aunt Jovana said, nodding at the head cook, who was now working away on my lump of dough. She smiled at the praise from her mistress, but not as brightly as she had when Etan said he loved her.

"I'd really like to," I said quietly, hoping this woman could see I was only trying to help.

She didn't respond but kept kneading, her hands bigger than any man's I'd ever seen. I looked around, trying to find another way to occupy myself. I went over to the flour to start measuring out more for myself. It was unfortunate that the massive bag was right beside Etan. I stood there for a minute, floundering.

"It's four," he said.

"I know that," I lied, digging the cup they'd used to measure into the bag. "If you know so much, why don't you come and help me?"

"Because it's more fun to watch you struggle, obviously."

I huffed, picking up my bowl and taking it back to the table. I stood there, looking at the other ingredients and trying to remember what I was supposed to get next. Water? Eggs? I found myself standing still in a room of activity. Even Scarlet, whose dough looked worse than mine, was getting patient instruction from one of the under cooks.

Etan's words told me what everyone else's actions already had: I wasn't welcome here. It didn't matter if our goal was to feed people who had nothing, my contributions weren't wanted. When I looked to people for help, our eyes only met briefly before they returned to their task, ignoring me.

I set the bowl down and wordlessly backed toward the stairs. The only person who might have noticed was Etan, but it didn't matter; no one came after me.

I tried not to cry as I scraped the wet flour from my arms into the washing bowl in my room. I'd been able to accept that I was going to be seen as *other* by the people of Isolte. What was unexpected was the aggression that came along with how that otherness was perceived. I hated it.

The tears came as I felt the Isoltens' distaste for me hit my heart over and over and over. Despite being with my only living family, I felt lonelier than I'd ever thought I could. It was a unique and unnecessary cruelty added on top of what everyone in the house knew: I'd lost everything.

But then another wave of tears came, flooding into the first, for a different reason.

Yes, I'd come to love a man from Isolte. I loved his family. I loved their queen. But I only loved them because I knew them. I'd laughed at Scarlet's clothes the first day she walked into the Great Room, and I'd disliked Valentina for being as typically standoffish as I knew Isoltens to be. I loved them now, but I'd judged them on first sight. I'd thought myself more stylish, wiser. I'd thought myself better.

I was only receiving what I'd happily handed out. Maybe they didn't know about it, and maybe it wasn't as blunt as this, but it was just as shameful.

And when I thought about it all, one of two things was absolutely true: either I deserved to be treated this way, or no one did. Ever.

I wished I had Silas to talk to. Ever the peacemaker, ever the thinker, Silas would have known what to do. I wiped at my tears and closed my eyes.

"What would you say?" I whispered to the air. "How would you patch this together?"

There was no answer, but I knew with a strange certainty that he wouldn't want me to hide. I lifted my chin and walked the long path back down the servants' stairs. I could feel the heat of the kitchen long before I arrived, inhaling the delicious scent of baking bread.

The first set of eyes I saw were Etan's, and they were painted with surprise.

"Ah, Hollis! There you are. We were . . . Are you quite well?" Aunt Jovana asked.

I shot a desperate look at Scarlet, who made excuses for me. "I sometimes cry without warning myself. It's been hard since . . . since . . ."

"Of course. Here, Hollis, come back to the table. Nothing eases your own pains like helping lift those of others."

I moved closer at Aunt Jovana's suggestion, taking my place again by Enid, her massive hands still a little intimidating.

"I think you might be right. Miss Enid," I said, looking up to the woman, "seeing as this is my family now, I really ought to learn how to do this properly. Will you show me again?"

She didn't smile, didn't even say yes. She picked up another bowl and set it in front of me, repeating her instructions from before. Delia Grace had always made it clear I was an awful student; it was still true. But I watched Enid's hands with stubborn intent. If she was going to show me, begrudgingly or not, I was going to learn.

And Etan stayed the entire time, never lifting a finger, never saying a word, but watching as if he was waiting for me to make a mistake. I didn't think I made one, but no one said one way or the other, and that felt good enough for one day.

I'd been so determined to prove myself, I stayed in the kitchens through the first batches of bread finishing. By the time we were moving the last bowls of dough to proof, a few of the women who worked on the Northcotts' land were making their way to the back door of the kitchen to fetch their bread.

As Aunt Jovana had promised, the gap in the trees now made sense to me. It provided a direct path for those who needed their master's help without disrupting the pristine front lands, which, for the sake of their status, would have been expected to be maintained and private. It was a way around that expectation and so very thoughtful.

Aunt Jovana took her time with each person who came, asking questions as she handed out bread. She knew names, knew stories. She checked on the children and made promises to stop by if anyone mentioned a particular problem. I watched in hushed awe.

"Surprised?" Etan asked, his eyes on his mother as she handed out food and wisdom.

"Yes," I admitted, observing as her hands clasped those of a woman in dull brown clothes, looking at her as if any gap in their rank was imagined. "But I shouldn't be. I'm not sure I know anyone as gentle as your parents. It makes me wonder how they managed to produce someone as angry as you."

"I'm not angry; I'm careful."

"You're a pain," I told him.

He nodded. "I know it."

I risked peeking up at him. There was a quiet resignation in his face that I didn't understand.

"You could easily change that," I offered.

"I could. But not for you," he said with a sigh. "We all have to make sacrifices. I must watch you like a hawk, Mother must work herself to the bone, and my father? Did you know it's his birthday? But there won't be any celebration."

I moved in front of him to get his full attention. "It's his birthday?"

"Yes."

"Then why in the world are we not making a special meal? Or dancing? Or anything?"

"Because there are bigger issues at hand than a party." Etan's tone implied I was an idiot for not seeing that.

"In a family where people die too soon, I can't think of much more important than celebrating one of us making it another year," I shot back.

Something in those eyes, those cold eyes that had been

watching me so closely, shifted. He looked like, perhaps, he agreed with me.

"What's the big tradition in Isolte? Silas and I never made it to a birthday, so I don't know."

Etan huffed. "Sweets. We make little cakes to wish someone a year filled with sweetness."

I nodded. "Well, we're in a kitchen, so that's perfect." I looked around the room until I found the wide hands of the head cook. "Miss Enid," I began, getting her attention, "did you know it's Lord Northcott's birthday?"

"I did."

"Then will you please help me make the appropriate sweets for him? Whatever the traditional ones are?"

She looked to Etan, then smirked at me. "Did you not have enough work for one day?"

"Not enough to keep me from celebrating someone I care about. So . . . if you please."

She shook her head. "Five cups of flour. I'll get the sugar."

I bounced into action, thrilled. Was I a good baker? Absolutely not. But I was exceptionally gifted at making merry, and that was exactly what I was going to do.

SEVEN

We were all in the dining room, ready to surprise Uncle Reid. We'd gotten more flowers from the garden for the table, lit extra candles around the room, and even had one of the servants who was handy with a lute come in and play. It was positively festive, and all we needed was our guest of honor.

When I heard his footsteps, I was nearly jumping with giddiness. Etan was shaking his head, but he almost looked like he was pleased. Maybe not. He wasn't the easiest to read.

"Surprise!" we yelled when Uncle Reid came around the corner, and he clutched his heart and smiled as he took in the room and his family.

"I told you I didn't want a fuss," he said as he walked to his seat, though his protest was half-hearted.

"Happy birthday, Father," Etan said.

"Thank you, son," he said, clapping his back as he came around. "You really shouldn't have."

"It was Hollis's idea," Aunt Jovana claimed.

I smiled. "Don't worry. Enid did the better part of the baking, so they shouldn't be too bad," I said, pointing to the pile of little cakes on a plate at the center of the table.

We all sat down, and Uncle Reid was grinning. "I suppose it's nice to have something to be happy about. Thank you all."

"Have a sweet, my love. To send you sweetly into another year," Aunt Jovana said, gesturing for him to pick one up.

Uncle Reid sighed, but there was no weight to it. He was smiling as he looked around the table at our small party. Finally, he reached out to grab the first one. He took a bite and rolled his eyes at how delicious it must have tasted.

"And now we all take one, too, so we're part of the sweet year," Mother whispered to me.

I reached out with the rest of the table, accidentally hitting both Mother's and Etan's hand as I took one of the little cakes. Even though I'd contributed to making them, I didn't know what it was exactly that made them so rich. Whatever it was, it tasted like heaven on earth.

"Mmm," I sighed, talking with my mouth full. "I could get used to these. Whose birthday is next? I can't wait to have these again."

"I think it's Scarlet," Mother said.

Scarlet, who was devouring her sweets, only nodded.

"Birthdays are the best," I said, taking another bite. "In

Coroa, we hold hands and dance around the person. Growing up it was just Mother and Father, but when we were at the castle, it was dozens of people. It was nice to be in the center of so many happy faces."

"Well, this is Isolte," Etan said firmly. "This is what *we* do."

After the uncomfortable silence, I broke it with a simple, "I know."

"Then adjust. If you're going to stay here, then you need to let go of Coroa."

It was clear the whole party wanted the subject to drop. But I wondered if any subject would ever simply drop between the two of us. I took a deep breath and went in.

"When your cousins moved to Coroa, did you expect them to give up everything they knew? All of their traditions?"

"Completely different," he replied quickly. "That was a family group, *and* they weren't going to stay forever—"

"Silas most certainly was!"

"—and you're alone, and, unless we get lucky, you're stuck here."

"Etan," Mother hissed.

"You cannot possibly tell me you're thankful *another* person has been dragged into this!" he shouted. "Furthermore, half our issues would be resolved if her kind would simply—"

"My *kind*?" I shouted, standing and sending the chair back behind me.

"Your people slaughter ours without a second thought.

Do you know how insufferable it is that you're under my roof?"

"Etan, we've been over this," Uncle Reid interjected resolutely.

"You act as if Isolte has never started an attack," I said coldly. "When it comes to wars between our countries, they've been exclusively instigated by you. Perhaps these skirmishes along the border are different, but are you not man enough to admit that Isolte carries some of the blame for the unrest?"

He stood himself, raking his fingers through his hair, a mad smile on his face. "You are so spoiled! Do you think wars that happened more than a hundred years ago have anything to do with what's happening *now*? Do you have any grasp of how many villages your king has burned?"

"*My* king? *Your* king burned your family, and you dare speak against *me*?!"

"Yes, and I will continue to do so until the day you leave or become an Isolten! Which, by the way, will *never* happen."

"Have I not done enough?" I asked, throwing my hands wide. "I married an Isolten. I left Coroa. I have come to be with my family, which I consider you part of, and you still—"

"You are *not* my family," he insisted, pointing his finger at me. "All you are is the girl who got *this close* to Jameson's bed. Didn't you hear a thing they said at the border? They think he's trying to get into the country. Why? Because he's lost his mind over you, for reasons I cannot begin to fathom.

And why wouldn't I believe you'd help him? Why would I trust you with my secrets when, at any minute, you could go running back to that man?"

I stared at him, feeling my gaze coming out dark and cold. "Don't. Move."

I left the room quickly, hurrying up the stairs and into my room. I grabbed what I'd come for and dashed back down, arms heavy. They were talking in my absence, quietly but forcefully. I couldn't make out much beyond Etan's unswerving refusal to apologize. I marched to stand across from Etan and tossed the entire bag of gold I'd brought with me at his chest. It hit him hard and he stumbled back into his chair, several coins spilling to the floor.

"Goodness, Hollis," Aunt Jovana said. "Where in the world did you get so much money?"

Etan was still looking down into his lap, shocked, but he finally dared to look at me.

"That is what I could carry of my widow's fund. This is what's given to every noblewoman in Coroa when they lose their husband. And now it's yours, you pig. Use it to raise whatever army you need, bribe whoever you have to. From this moment on, Jameson Barclay's money is funding your pursuit for justice, and it came at *my* hands. Do not forget it."

"Hollis," Mother whispered. I held up a hand, stopping her, unable to tear my eyes away from Etan Northcott.

"I have never said this to another living soul . . . but I hate you," I breathed.

He smirked humorlessly. "I've said this to too many people

to count, but I mean it all the same: I hate *you*."

"Etan," Uncle Reid said calmly. "Apologize."

"Don't bother. I've been lied to enough. Do excuse me." I turned and left, head high, hoping I was still holding on to some trace of the lady I once was.

There was an eruption of discussion in my wake, and I hated that they were arguing because of me.

I was proud of myself for not crying until I got to my room. I just couldn't understand his anger, as if I'd done something to him with my own two hands. I hadn't.

I sat there for a long time with my frustrations and rage and sorrow, and I came to a simple conclusion: I'd made a mistake.

I never should have come to Isolte.

In three short days, my presence had torn holes in what was left of a great family. I had exhausted what little I could contribute to their planning. I was not welcome by the staff, would surely be judged to my family's detriment by any neighbors, and, after so many years of being talked down to, I couldn't take another word from Etan's mouth.

I needed to leave.

There was no way they would let me go if I asked, so I had to run. It was easy enough to get my things together and into the bags I'd brought them in; I had so little that was truly my own.

I penned a quick letter of apology and left it on my bed. Once it was late enough that everyone would certainly be asleep or at least in their quarters, I padded downstairs, heading to the kitchen using the servants' stairs.

I waited at the door, looking to make sure the room was empty. Once satisfied, I started walking through, only to hear a gasp behind me. I turned, seeing there was a girl against the wall by the door I'd missed in my search.

"Oh. It's you, miss. Can I help you?"

"You did not see me. Do you understand?"

I didn't wait for her to agree but moved to the back door, taking a direct path to the stables I'd seen on the tour Aunt Jovana had given me. But was she my aunt anymore? If I left? I shook the thought away. Madge was in there, resting, but she perked up the moment she smelled me.

"Hey, girl. Want to see Coroa again? Let me find a saddle."

It took a little hunting to find where everything was kept, but Madge was ready when I placed the saddle and bags across her back. I pulled the hood of my cape up and slid on gloves, hoping to be as anonymous as possible; I didn't know how I'd be received on either side of the border.

We quietly trotted around the front of the house to head to the road that was the only link I knew to get to the border. On the long path to the manor, I paused, looking back. It felt like I was driving a spike down the center of my heart. And then, because I couldn't help the sorrow, I cried. I'd lost too many people against my will, and it was a different pain entirely to lose them because I was choosing to walk away.

I cupped my hand across my mouth and stared at the house for a minute, tears running down my face.

"Please forgive me," I whispered. "I don't know what else to do."

I turned and moved into the night.

EIGHT

THE MOON WASN'T NEARLY BRIGHT enough to light the way, so I slowed my horse to a walk. The journey and the night were both incredibly long. I wished I'd been smart enough to think of bringing a dagger, or anything that might have lent me some security. In fact, I was starting to wish I'd remained an ignorant lady in the palace, or that I'd listened to Mother and stayed in Coroa in the first place . . . but no. Even if I couldn't bring myself to finish what I'd started, I didn't regret a single second of what I'd done.

It took me a while to notice there was a horse and rider in the distance who looked to be following me. I could tell they were moving faster than I was, and if I didn't do something, they'd be upon me within a minute. I did not want to come across a thief or worse alone in the dark.

My instinct was to leave the trail, to hide. But if they had seen me, that was it. My second thought was to go into a full gallop and try to outrun them, which seemed unlikely with how poorly I knew the roads. Before I could decide, a voice rang out.

"Hollis! Hollis, wait!"

I pulled the reins and came to a stop. "Etan? Is that you?" I steadied my horse, my heart racing, and watched him approach.

"Going somewhere?" he asked casually when he caught up.

I shook my head. "How did you even know I was gone?"

He sighed, unable to look me in the eye. "I saw you go."

Of course he did. His room was next to mine, and they both looked out upon the front of the manor. Why hadn't I thought to make sure he was asleep before setting off?

"I'm not going back," I said hotly. "I don't know what's waiting for me in Coroa, but I'm sure you'll agree that it will be better for everyone if I just go." I hated that I felt so very close to tears as I went on. "As you've pointed out many times, I'm not an Isolten, and I'm not really family. It will be better for everyone if I just . . . disappear."

"No, it won't," he said. "You're coming back with me. You'd never make it to Coroa on your own anyway."

"I can figure it out."

"Hollis, you can hardly figure out your wardrobe. Turn around!"

"You should be rejoicing!" I replied bitterly. "You've been pushing me out of the house since the second I arrived, after all. And anyway, if you saw me leave, then why in the world did you let me get this far before trying to stop me?"

"Because I *wanted* you to go. Obviously." He was still looking away, shaking his head. "And then I realized I couldn't possibly let that happen."

I narrowed my eyes. "And why is that?" I shot back sarcastically.

"Because I know you, Hollis." He finally looked at me, his eyes stern.

The words were eerily similar to something that Silas had said once, words that made me see I needed to run away with him, even if it led to my ruin. If Etan Northcott thought he was going to steal the memory of those words, he was mistaken.

"You may know many things, Etan Northcott, but you do not know me."

"Yes, I do," he insisted quietly. "I know that you have already had your fill of death. I know that you would rather live a long life alone in agony if it meant those you loved could walk the earth just a little while longer. I know . . ." He paused, swallowing hard. "I know that, even when you're miserable, you look out for other people. It's been years since I've seen my mother smile the way she did when you put flowers in her hair." He looked down, almost seeming ashamed. "And I know that you think that Aunt Whitley and Scarlet will forget you, that my parents will, too . . . but they won't."

Etan had seen right through my walls, to my poorly concealed fears. Tears stung at my eyes, so I didn't dare speak.

"I've already done everything you're thinking of doing," he told me. "And I built a wall between myself and my family. It makes it easier for them to bear not having me near. But you are different. You light up any room you're in, and if you are not there when they wake tomorrow, Hollis, they will all be defeated by it."

"They wo—"

"They will," he assured me. "Come home."

Home. What was home anymore? I certainly didn't know.

I looked at him, studying the seriousness in his eyes as he went on. "You do realize that, if you continue, I will just be sent to fetch you all the same, even if I have to follow you to the border. And while I appreciate your proclivity to heroism, that boldness will undoubtedly be wrung out of you there."

I sighed, knowing he was right. If I kept going, he'd only track me, and that would certainly end in disaster. If not for me, then for him. And I couldn't be the cause of more mourning.

Wordlessly, I urged Madge into a trot, heading back to the manor. "How will we make this work at the house?" I asked. "You can't stand me, and I'm not particularly fond of you myself."

"Easy. Self-control. Believe it or not, I have some. We will simply avoid speaking to one another unless we absolutely must. And as much as it pains me, I will drop all insults to Coroa and your unfortunate loyalty for the time being."

I sighed. "I just gave you every last penny I have. Is that

not enough to prove I'm with you?"

"To a point," he conceded. "But it's hard to forget that you were nearly queen."

"So there you have it," I said flatly. "You don't really trust me, and I don't trust you. How can I know you will keep your word, that you won't be arguing with me and belittling me all the time?"

He looked me dead in the eye. "I would hope by now that you know I never say things I don't mean."

The sound of our horses echoed in the night. "Well, I can't deny that. Fine. I will keep my distance, and I will avoid talking about anything in front of you that might tempt you to be an arse."

"Good luck there."

I smirked for a quick second before becoming serious again. "And please don't tell them I left."

"I won't."

We sank into silence, and I rode beside him all the way back to the manor. The sky was turning a beautiful pink, but I was worried with each new ray of sunshine that everyone would wake to discover that I'd attempted to abandon them.

"Hurry," Etan said, reading my thoughts. "If we cut through here, we can come up around the back of the manor."

He launched off the road, and I followed, springing into a gallop. Etan was a fair rider, nearly as steady as Jameson, which was saying something. After a sleepless night, it felt good to really move, to almost fly across the field. We ducked into a short line of trees, coming out into fields of grain where people were already hard at work.

As we rode past, men tipped their cloth hats and women curtsied, recognizing one of the landowners on sight. Etan greeted many by name in return.

"You put me to shame," I told him, and he looked over with questioning eyes. "I don't know a single person who worked our land. I wish I'd done better."

He shrugged. "You *can* do better. When you go back. Because you will one day, Hollis. Eventually, you will get your life back."

"We'll see."

I wasn't sure if I'd survive the month, so it was hard to make plans beyond that. Etan led me to a familiar row of trees. We went through the opening, and there was the back of the manor and the path leading to the kitchen.

"Do you think anyone's up yet?"

"No," he said with a yawn. "But we'll take the servants' stairs just in case."

He tapped on the kitchen window, waving at whoever was in there. Someone came and opened the door for us, and we got a few shocked looks from the cooking staff.

"Don't get any ideas," Etan said, playfully wagging a finger at them. "This was a rescue mission, and I expect you all to keep our presence to yourselves. There's enough going on as it is." Etan's tone was so lazy that it hardly felt like a command, yet I knew everyone in that room would obey.

"Oh, thank goodness," a voice said, and I turned to see

the girl who'd caught me leaving.

"Sorry I put such a secret on you," I said. "I won't again."

Etan watched the quick interaction, looking as if he'd put the final stroke on a painting. "Let's go, Hollis."

He turned to go up the stairs, but only made it one step before wheeling back around to the room. "And by the way," he added, wagging that same finger in the air, "as of this morning, when Lady Hollis holds up her cup, it is filled. If she rings a bell, it gets answered. For better or worse, she's . . . part of the family, and she'll be treated as such."

His gaze swept across the room, meeting every pair of eyes with absolute seriousness.

In that moment, I knew he meant to keep his word. Even if he hated me, he wouldn't tear me down again.

"Don't worry, sir," Enid said, waddling across the room, her arms full of some unrecognizable fruit. "We'd all come to that conclusion yesterday." She looked at me. "I think you were right to make them celebrate the master's birthday. He's a good man."

"He is," I agreed. "One of the best."

"Ah, Enid, my love!" Etan said, blowing a kiss at her. "I knew you'd never let me down."

"Out you go!" she ordered with a laugh, and we scurried up the thin back stairs, trying not to make them creak, but not knowing how to avoid it.

When we came out on the second floor, we had to round a few corners before coming to the wing that housed our rooms. It seemed we'd gone undetected.

"I know it's a challenge even when you're rested, but go and put yourself together," Etan said sarcastically. "It's going to be a long day."

I crossed my arms. "Very funny. For goodness' sake, don't you shave?"

I went around him and into my room, amazed that we'd actually done it. We'd gotten back home, and no one knew, and we could just keep moving forward. I tore up the letter I'd written the night before and threw the scraps into the fireplace for kindling. Maybe I'd tell them of my moment of weakness one day when it was far behind us and we'd won our battle. For now, I needed to splash some water on my face and change into a clean dress. It was going to be an exhausting day.

NINE

I WENT DOWN TO BREAKFAST with bleary eyes, fully expecting to have an opportunity to practice my newly made bargain with Etan. Only, he wasn't there.

"Are you all right?" Mother wondered, looking me over.

"Yes. Why? What's wrong?" I asked a little too quickly.

"No reason. You just seem tired."

"Didn't sleep well," I admitted.

"Well, we'll take it easy today," Aunt Jovana insisted. "I have several letters to write, and I desperately need your and Scarlet's help. If Etan's right, we have some dear friends to inform of . . . recent events." She did her best to actually avoid the words. I followed her lead.

"I have excellent handwriting," I told her. "It was the one thing in my academic career Delia Grace praised me for."

"Oh! That reminds me!" Aunt Jovana stood up and rushed

over to a side table. "This came late last night. I didn't want to wake you. I hope it's nothing too urgent." She made a face like she was questioning her choice while I was counting my blessings she'd made the choice she had.

Across the front of the folded paper, the name of Varinger Hall was crossed out, and the words *Northcott, Isolte* were written beneath it, as that was all anyone at my home had to go on. I didn't recognize the handwriting.

I broke the unfamiliar seal, going directly to the end to see who it was from. "Nora!"

"Really?" Scarlet asked. "What does she say? I mean, I'm sorry; I don't want to intrude."

I looked up from my letter just in time to see Etan walking into the room. The little snake had shaved, and he plopped himself into his chair with a smirk on his face, daring me to say something.

There was a beat of tension at the table as everyone waited for us to continue our fight where they assumed we'd left off. But we'd made our peace, however fragile it might be, and it was time to carry on as best we could.

"I have no secrets from you," I said to the room at large, hoping Etan took note. I cleared my throat and went to the letter. "'Dear Hollis, for goodness' sake, come back.'"

I had to pause and laugh, and it lifted my spirits to see Scarlet smile at that greeting. "'I don't intend to make light of things. I know that you have been through something unspeakable, and it's still unbelievable to me that your parents are gone. I imagine you need comfort right now, and if you were close, I would be that for you. I hope you're finding it in some way at your family home. All the same, I so wish you were here.

"'I don't think I realized before how much joy you brought to the palace. Delia Grace is doing her best to fill your shoes (ah, your shoes!).'" I stopped to giggle, but only Mother and Scarlet understood the joke. "'But she's no Hollis. I miss your jokes and your laughter . . .'" I had to pause and take a breath. "'. . . and I hope you miss mine, too.

"'I don't mean to take digs at Delia Grace. I think we always knew she was ambitious, but the way she's wormed her way into the king's affections has me . . . uncomfortable. She and I are still on speaking terms, and I have you to thank for that. But I worry how things will be if she's ever queen.'"

"What is it?" Mother asked, taking in the concern on my face.

"Nothing. . . . It's just, I knew Delia Grace always hoped to be on Jameson's arm. I wonder what it is she's doing that would make anyone raise eyebrows. And it makes me wonder about that soldier at the border who said he wasn't true to her. She had so many plans, knew how to play the game . . ." I went back to the letter.

"'Perhaps I'm worried for nothing. Perhaps I'm just tired of the tension of court.

"'Sometimes the king still talks of you. Someone will do something, and it will remind him of you, and he feels obligated to tell the story in full. How you . . .'" I blushed, giving myself away.

Etan scoffed. "No secrets, indeed."

I took a deep breath. "'How you kissed him in the room that held all the royal jewels.' Which isn't how that happened, by the way," I said, looking up again. "We were in *his* rooms, and he kissed me. 'And then that story will lead into how you used berries to paint your lips once. And then that story will lead into how you used berries as ammunition on me. I can see Delia Grace dying inside when he does it, which is part of what makes me nervous. She seems so uneasy, even with you gone.

"'Come visit us soon. Even if you have no intentions of winning the king over (which I'm still hoping for, I confess), I think it will set her at ease if you come and go and nothing happens. She will see you as our dear old joyful Hollis, and maybe we can all keep moving on. I don't know how your days are going, but I hope you will find time to write me soon and tell me of all your adventures. I'm not sure if you've stayed in contact with the Eastoffe family after what I heard happened, but if you are, please tell the Lady Scarlet I send my best dance steps her way.'" I looked up, seeing this single line brought tears to Scarlet's eyes. Happy ones. "'I wish you well, Hollis. Send me pretty words soon to light up court. Your friend and servant, Nora.'"

I folded the letter, feeling a little warmer inside. It wasn't exactly a positive update, but it was a comfort all the same. The maid came around, filling cups as the family reflected on the words Nora was kind enough to send.

"Idle gossip," Etan remarked.

"Not so," I countered. "It confirmed something for us."

He squinted at me as I continued. "People in Isolte don't know what happened to my family, but the people of Coroa do. Seeing as Quinten isn't their king, perhaps no one fears sharing the story there."

His shoulders slumped as he considered this. "You're right."

Uncle Reid stopped midchew to gape at his son.

And the maid poured ale into my cup.

And that all felt as warming as the letter had.

Uncle Reid cleared his throat, looking as if he wanted to preserve the rare peaceful moment between us. "What are your plans for the day, son?"

"Sleeping. Rotten night."

I was inclined to look around the table, to see if anyone was attempting to link his sleepless night to mine, and hoping that, if they did, they didn't draw the wrong conclusion. It was unlikely, as we had been at each other's throats last they knew. In the end, I only glanced at Scarlet, and I could see her mind was working, but I went back to my food, refusing to give her anything to feed that fire.

"When's the next bread day?" I asked, needing to get our minds on a new subject.

"Saturday," Aunt Jovana said. "Today my biggest tasks are those letters, and I've almost finished tailoring a dress for you, Hollis, that I'll need you to try on."

"Certainly."

"Son, would you be willing to come with me to visit the

Biermans today?" Uncle Reid asked. "Their oldest is talking of moving."

Up to this point, Etan's days had consisted of following me around like an obnoxious shadow, but it seemed today would finally be a change of pace. "Sure. I haven't seen him in ages. Where is Ash thinking of moving to? Is he planning not to farm anymore?"

The morning post had arrived, and a maid walked in with another letter and presented it to Uncle Reid as he answered Etan. "I don't think so. I think young Ash wants to try his hand at a new trade. It's making his parents nervous."

"*Young Ash*," Etan repeated with a smirk and a shake of his head. "We're the same age."

"Yes. Yes, you are."

As if he had no cares for whatever the letter might say, Uncle Reid continued giving his son a knowing smile as he reached up to take it. But both his and Etan's faces went dark at exactly the same moment, prompting me to speak.

"What is it?" I asked.

Etan sighed heavily, answering without breaking his eyes from the letter. "A royal seal."

TEN

"A royal seal?" Scarlet asked, her voice pitching higher. She was simultaneously swallowing and bracing herself.

Uncle Reid scanned the message quickly, sharing the news as he went.

"We are summoned to the palace. Prince Hadrian is getting married at the end of the week. There is to be a ball and a tournament with the wedding capping off the festivities." He sighed. "Well, that's that."

Everyone at the table looked dejected—or worse, terrified—but I sat up taller.

"This is great news!"

Etan's eyes were the first to look at me in disbelief. "How is our enemy finally managing to marry off his son and prolong their line a good thing?"

"You keep saying you'd have support if you had undeniable

proof. The best place you could ever find it would be in the castle. And we just got invited there."

Uncle Reid smirked while Etan sank in his chair, irritated again that I was right.

"Bravo, Hollis. That's the kind of attitude we all need to have. This trip is a great opportunity. We will listen to learn what those at court have heard, see what we can find ourselves, and gather our support. I fear this may be our last chance."

"What do you need from us?" Mother asked.

"Active hands and ears. Speak to everyone and try to learn if anyone's seen anything with their own eyes. Garner favor. We must be present and in the thick of everything. It will both make Quinten see us as submissive supporters and allow us room to finalize our plans. We also need to present a united front, to show that we are not broken despite our trials. To that end," he said, leaning forward and looking to me first, then Etan. "You will be escorting Hollis to every event."

I watched as Etan's jaw dropped. His eyes darted back and forth, clearly trying to muster up an excuse.

"Whatever you're thinking, let it go. Everyone is aware of your feelings toward Coroa. If you can be not just civil but *kind* to her, that will make a bigger statement about the unity of our family than any speech I could offer. So, you will be her escort, and I will hear nothing more about it."

He looked at me, and I stared back at him. Whatever peace we'd agreed to, this might stretch it past its breaking point.

But, seeing as we were on a mission here, I didn't think there was a way around the arrangement.

Etan's shoulders sagged. "Yes, Father."

Uncle Reid looked at me, and I merely nodded. "Good. We'll leave tomorrow, so you'd all best start packing."

I was gripped with panic, and I could feel my body getting tense over the prospect of walking into Quinten's home and court.

"Don't worry," Scarlet whispered. "I have dresses you can borrow."

I smiled and nodded, not even thinking about that. I was going to have to blend in, and there was little chance of that; tight-sleeved gowns were the least of my concerns.

I lay awake in bed for a long time. Even with the exhaustion from my escape attempt the night before, even with a comfortable fire, it was impossible to fall asleep. I worried, perhaps to an irrational degree, what it would be like to face King Quinten tomorrow.

Maybe it was my imagination, but I felt like I could hear Etan next door, pacing at times, then throwing himself on his bed before getting up again. Was he as anxious as I was? Or did the man just never settle?

I gasped a little at the knock on my door, sitting upright.

"Just me," Scarlet whispered. "See how startling it is?"

I giggled, pulling the blankets back for her to jump in. She lay down, but I stayed sitting up, resting my head on my knees.

"Perhaps we need a special sound. I could hoot like an owl or something before I come in," I proposed.

"Yes. That will be lovely. Very noble of you," she offered. "I figured you'd be awake. You all right?"

"No. I'm not. I'm so tired, but my mind is just . . ." It was all such a tangle, but when the words started coming out, so did the truth. "I'm afraid, Scarlet. Unlike you, this is all very new to me. You've always had this secret in your pocket, this knowledge of who you are and what it means in this big sweeping story of your kingdom. I'm just a girl who happened to fall in love with a boy . . . and now we're here, and I don't know what I'm supposed to do.

"I'm not Isolten; I don't see how anyone would entrust me—a *stranger*—with any vital information. And King Quinten disliked me from the start. I have this fear that any role I might have to play in getting justice for Silas is useless. I'm not as brash as Etan or as keenly observant as you. Mother and Uncle Reid are planners, and Aunt Jovana is this quiet sense of calm over everything. What about me?" I asked, finally seeming to put all the jumbled thoughts in my head to a point.

What about me?

Should I have kept running last night despite Etan's protests? Should I never have come at all? Was there even anything I could do to help us find a solution?

"What, you want to know your role in all this?" she asked.

"Yes! Desperately!"

Scarlet sat up, looking deep into my eyes. "Too bad,

because I don't know." The matter-of-factness in her face made me want to laugh, which was good as that seemed to be her goal. "Hollis, all I can tell you is that I believe you're here for a reason. And maybe we don't know what it is today, but I'm certain that whatever happens, we'll need you."

"You think?" I asked, finally lying down.

"I do," she said, joining me.

We were quiet for a long time, lost in our own thoughts. I liked that about Scarlet, that I could be silent with her.

"I'm trained, Hollis," she said out of nowhere. "Since I was old enough to carry a sword, I've learned to swing one. But when . . ." Her lips started trembling, and I knew then that she was telling the story we all thought she'd never tell. She swallowed and kept going. "When they came in, I couldn't move to save my life. I can remember that very thought going through my head: if you want to live, you have to move. And I couldn't."

I watched as she fidgeted with the edge of the blankets, trying to tame her thoughts.

"They walked in without fanfare. The first few people fell without any sort of fear or anticipation because they were *so quiet*. No one started running until a few people realized what was happening and started to scream.

"Hollis, I know it was only a few minutes, but it felt so slow. Every day new pieces of the picture fall into place, new memories. Father yelled at Silas to run. But Silas . . . he wouldn't go. Father grabbed a sword off the wall and went into the fray, and Silas followed right behind him. They took down at least two men that I saw before . . ." She had to pause. "Father went down first. I looked away and then saw Sullivan was jumping in front of me on my right."

She shook her head. "It's like they didn't think a single stab was enough for him. The way they . . . I don't think I can tell you about all of that."

"It's all right. You don't have to share anything you don't want to." I reached out for her hand, and she gave it to me, gripping me with all her might. She took a moment to let out a sob, wiping at her face with the back of her hand. I wondered if she would stop then, she seemed so pained by the memories. But she didn't.

"I didn't see what happened to your parents. Honestly, I kept looking for *you*. I didn't know you and Mother weren't in there. My eyes just kept darting across the room, feet planted to the floor. I have pieces of images. A neck. Clutched hair. I remember someone threw a vase. Blood. So much blood.

"They started pouring oil on the floor and ripping down all the tapestries we'd worked so hard to clean and hang. I still can't remember when I started seeing the fire.

"And then, suddenly, there was someone in front of me, gripping me by my arms. I remember looking down at his hands, thinking they were too big for any human to have. I had bruises from the way he held me later, but I didn't even feel them at the time. I waited for the sword. But he just kept looking into my eyes, and after studying me for a minute, he grabbed another man in black. The second man looked at me and nodded, and the man who had me by the shoulders shoved me toward the door. After he pushed me, my legs worked enough to get me to the front of the manor. I tripped over Saul on the way out. He was so still, but I didn't see him until I was on the ground and looked back to see what I'd caught my foot on. I reached back to shake him, but he was already gone.

"By then I had to crawl. I crawled through the front doors and down the steps and into the bushes. My head started racing. I was alone. They let me live, and I couldn't figure out why. I was prepared to die, Hollis. I always knew it could come. It's the living when everyone else has left that makes it so hard."

I nodded. "That I understand."

Her hands were finally warming up in mine. "My mind was a wreck, but I tried to make a plan. I was asking myself where I could go, what I could do if I was all alone now. I figured I'd have to go back to Isolte. No one looking like me was going to stay in Coroa peacefully on their own. So, I figured I'd steal a horse, go north, and sneak back into Isolte through Bannir. I could live in the country, and no one would know I was an Eastoffe, and I could just grow old. Since I was a little girl, Hollis, I never knew if I'd have a chance to grow old. I am determined now. I will."

"Of course you will. By the end of this, we'll have answers, justice. That man will never do this to another living soul," I vowed.

She kissed my hands, still clutched tightly to hers. "That's why we need you, Hollis. That's your part. When you decided you wanted to marry a king, you made it happen. When you changed your mind and wanted a boy from Isolte, you made that happen. When we told you to stay put and you didn't like it, you made us take you. You tend to work impossible things together. Don't overlook that," she said.

I closed the gap between us, embracing her. "How lucky was I to get you?" I said. "Stay here tonight, please. After hearing that and with all that's on my mind, I don't think I could manage without you."

She nodded, and I moved back, making space for us to comfortably rest. I held on to Scarlet's hand, thinking of everything she'd just told me, of what she'd seen. If she kept remembering things, I wondered what the story would sound like if she told me again in a year. It was hard to imagine a memory like that growing, and it was even harder to imagine that she was the only one carrying it.

I wasn't sure if she was right, if I tended to make things happen, but if Scarlet thought I could, then I was certainly willing to try.

ELEVEN

Uncle Reid had been very serious when he'd said Etan would be my escort for the entirety of the trip. As I went to board the coach, he led me to the one behind it.

"They both only seat four, and you and Etan need to make your peace before we get there," he instructed.

"But we have!"

He smiled. "Well, you need to make it better."

I held his arm to climb in and sighed, thinking I could go a lifetime without a trip like the one I was about to face. Not a minute later, Etan lumbered in, shaking the entire carriage and forcing me to grip the windowsill as he settled beside me.

I gawked at him. "You are aware the seat across from me is vacant, and you can have it all to yourself, yes?"

He ticked his head up slightly, not looking at me as he

spoke. "Riding backward makes me feel sick. Of course, you are free to move anytime you like."

I sighed. "Actually, it makes me sick, too."

He looked over at me, and it was strange to find we had something in common.

"My mother thought I was lying, making myself ill to get out of going back and forth to Keresken. Took her years to figure out I was telling the truth," I admitted.

He smirked, almost unwillingly. "I liked to sit on my mother's lap during rides as a child, and she loves facing backward. Likes knowing where she's been. Seeing as Isoltens are constantly dabbling in new medicines, she tried so many different capsules made for traveling sicknesses, and even some sleeping solutions, but nothing worked. Eventually, I got big enough that I had to sit on my own, and everything was fine after that."

With those stories shared, we lapsed into silence. It wasn't necessarily a comfortable silence. I was aware of Etan's breaths and his movements, aware of when he was watching me, as if he was still trying to piece me together. I thought maybe I'd earned his trust . . . perhaps I was wrong.

The first hour of our trip consisted of exactly four words. The carriage hit a rock and threw me sideways into him. Instinctively, he reached out to grab my arm and keep me from falling. I said, "Thank you" and he said, "You're welcome."

But somewhere in the second hour of our trip, Etan cleared his throat.

"What were your parents' names again?"

"What?"

"Well, you are supposedly part of the family now. Oughtn't I know? Besides, I'm sure at least one person will need proof you are in fact a lady."

I shook my head. "My mother was *Lady* Claudia Cart Brite, and my father was *Lord* Noor Brite. They were both descendants of long lines in Coroan aristocracy, and had they had sons, the line would be . . . going still."

"What's wrong?" he asked, bending to look me in the eye.

"Nothing. It's . . . I only just realized the Brite line is dead. My parents are gone, and I'm an Eastoffe. When I was going to marry Jameson, I didn't think about it so much. What son could give them such a gift? What son could have made them royalty? But there are no sons, and I am not queen, and it's ended . . . because of me."

It was one of the many deaths I couldn't reconcile myself to. I now understood that the Darkest Knights were going to come for the Eastoffes one day whether I was with them or not. That was not the case for the rest of our company.

My parents, for instance, had been adamantly against my marrying Silas. It seemed to go even deeper than the fact he was both common and foreign, though I could never quite understand their reasoning. Whatever it was, it was enough to keep them from wanting to come to the ceremony, and had I not pleaded with them to, they might have been spared.

I felt such guilt over their deaths, guilt I couldn't quite

express because all my grief got tied up in Silas. But it was there, sharp and deep, and I had no way to make it right.

"How *did* all your plans to be queen come undone? It looked so painfully tied up when we came to visit," Etan commented offhandedly.

"It did, didn't it?" I replied in wonder. The crown had been so close. "It seems a pair of blue eyes knocked me off course." I smiled, lost in my memories. "Jameson . . . he was an adventure. It was like a game to master or a challenge to be met. But Silas felt like destiny. He felt like the world properly centering itself. I don't know if I have the right words for it."

Etan shook his head. "And now that he's gone? Would you call that destiny still?"

His tone wasn't teasing or even unkind, but genuinely curious: What did I make of a love story that barely had a first page?

"I would. Maybe our story is bigger than us."

He considered this. "Maybe it is."

My voice dropped. "It doesn't mean I don't ache for him, though. I keep fearing I'll forget what his eyes looked like. Or the sound of his laugh. I worry that everything will go away . . . and then I wonder whether something is wrong with me if I force myself to hold on."

I hadn't meant to share so much, but it was true. And it hurt. For a minute, there was nothing but the sound of the wheels spinning, spinning, spinning. Just when I thought Etan was letting me in, he decided to ignore my pain.

Finally, he coughed.

"That, madam, is a fear I understand."

I dared to look over at him, but his face was squarely focused outside the window, so I couldn't read it.

"Four years ago, I lost Tenen. Last year, Micha. Two weeks before we were forced to visit Coroa, I lost Vincent and Giles."

"Family?"

"Friends," he corrected me gently, turning to look at me. "Friends so close I called them family. And now I am the last of us to live . . . I can't imagine why. I feel like I should have died a long time ago." He shook his head. "Everyone I care about dies. It's one of the reasons I still can't understand Silas. I was almost *angry* at him when I heard about your wedding."

"I beg your pardon?"

He shook his head. "It's not because he sank so low as to marry a Coroan," he said mockingly, though I could tell that, for once, there was no venom behind the word. "After *everything* our family has been through, I can't think of anything more reckless than to drag someone else into it. I couldn't believe he married *anyone*. You will never catch me as a groom."

"Then I will say a prayer of thanks that you are sparing some girl such a fate."

He chuckled, amused.

"Not everyone you love dies," I countered softly. "Your parents are still here."

He gave me a sad smile. "But they're the last ones left. You're new to this; you have no idea how many people we've lost. And if you think I'm not worried that my parents are walking straight into their coffins today, you are sadly mistaken."

I swallowed. "Surely he wouldn't murder us at a wedding."

Etan shrugged. "I think the king wants us to witness his greatest triumph first, but that doesn't make me comfortable. If we can leave immediately after the ceremony, that's what I'd prefer. Of course, I am at my father's command."

"Perhaps I could say I'm under the weather and need to retreat home, and, seeing as you are my escort for everything . . ."

He perked up. "That may be the best idea you've had to date."

"I have plenty of good ideas." I sat up, crossing my arms.

"Ah, yes. Jilting a king, running off in the middle of the night. You're brilliant," he teased.

"You willingly run into border disputes and alienate your family . . . I hardly think you have the room to criticize my judgment."

"And yet I will." He smiled, quite pleased with himself.

I shook my head, looking back out the window. Always so sure of himself, always so quick with his words. Etan was positively insufferable.

The Isolten countryside gave way to small houses and then larger ones, and I let out an audible gasp when we hit the road paved with stones and our carriage was bolted up onto the strange and rocky pathway.

"The stones are common here," Etan said. "The coast is teeming with them, so you'll see the same ones everywhere, especially here in the capital."

"Are we already there?" I asked, poking my head out to see.

"Almost. And I'd come back in if I were you. Just because we're nearing the castle doesn't mean there aren't dangerous people out there. In fact, I'd wager we're getting closer to more."

"Oh." I pulled myself into my seat, trying to see what I could without being too obvious about it. There were wide two-story houses set close together with only enough gardening space before them to grow very small patches of flowers. They shortly gave way to crammed-together homes that seemed to go up and up. There were shops on the bottom level, many with glass and lead windows, showing off the wares inside.

A woman beat out a rug; a man pulled an unwilling cow down an alley. Some very dirty children ran around in naked feet, while I saw at least one tidy daughter, gripping her mother's hand as they moved up the road.

"Do the poor live here?"

"Some. Lots of people live in the city in general. Some prefer the labor of the tanner or the seamstress to a field. But it's cramped and, as you can see, not very clean. Still, with the various industries popping up, it's good work."

"It smells."

He sighed. "Yes, Miss High and Mighty, it does. But it gets better closer to the castle."

A few minutes passed, and Etan pointed out his window, motioning for me to come over and see. "Chetwin Palace. Just there."

I looked out to take in the most foreboding building I'd ever seen. The roofs were pitched at a very steep angle, perhaps to withstand the frequent snows, and they were covered in some dark, shiny material. The stones used to build the palace were the same ones used on the roads: woven through with veins of white, which were somehow unsettling when I compared them to the warmer-toned stones used in Coroa.

It was intimidating, to be sure. And yet, somehow, I couldn't help but be moved by its strange beauty as we approached. As if reading my mind, Etan spoke as we turned onto the palace drive.

"I used to be completely awestruck when we came up to the palace as children. The soaring towers, the flags whipping in the wind. No wonder people think that kings are gods. Look at their homes."

He gestured a hand across all of it, as if there wasn't a word big enough to encompass the grandeur. He was right, of course, and it was both wondrous and, somehow, terrifying.

"You know how you feel about marriage? That's how I feel about crowns. You couldn't pay me any sum of money that would draw me close to one again . . . but, all that said, I loved Keresken Castle. I was always finding a new corner that held some beauty I'd never seen. And the way the light falls through the stained glass in the throne room . . . it left me breathless. Still does."

He smiled. "If you could build your own castle . . ."

"Stained glass everywhere," I sighed. "Obviously."

"A huge garden."

"Yes!" I agreed. "With a maze."

"A maze?" he asked skeptically.

"They're quite amusing. And sweet-smelling flowers."

"A circular throne room."

I squinted. "Circular?"

"Yes," he insisted, his voice implying this was an obvious necessity. "If a room is rectangular, there's a head and a foot. Clear ranking. If it's round, everyone looks to the center. Everyone is equally welcome."

I smiled. "Then it must have a circular throne room."

The carriage came to a stop, and Etan gave me an encouraging but sober look. "Are you ready?"

"I think so. Yes."

"Very well." He hopped out quickly, kicking up gravel in his wake.

And I took his hand with what, I was surprised to find, felt like a very genuine smile.

TWELVE

Etan escorted me to the rest of the family as they, too, were exiting their coach. Mother was rubbing her back, and the tension in Scarlet's shoulders was unmistakable.

"They look like different people," I whispered to Etan.

"We all are at the castle," he replied. "You try not to change. They'll need you."

I nodded as I came up to Scarlet and embraced her.

"Was it awful?" she asked quietly.

"Well, there was no bloodshed, so I'll call it a victory."

She chuckled, and we both turned to Mother. "What's first?" I asked.

It was Uncle Reid who answered. "We present ourselves to the king." He turned to offer Aunt Jovana his arm, and right behind them, Mother and Scarlet took one another's hand.

"Right now?" I asked Etan under my breath.

He adjusted the dagger on his waist. I hadn't noticed it in the carriage. "Better to get a sense of his mood and intentions straightaway. And it may even his temper when he sees Aunt Whitley and Scarlet alone. Best to do it right away."

I smoothed down my dress, the motion about as difficult as I'd expected with the draping Isolten sleeves, and swallowed. It was always going to come to this. Eventually, I would have to look that man in the face. I had to be respectful and silent, all the while knowing I was staring into the eyes of the person who had ordered the death of my husband. I found myself drawing in short, staggered breaths as I realized how close I was to my enemy.

"What is it?" Etan asked, his eyes never actually coming down to me but instead surveying the crowd.

"Etan, I don't think I can do this," I whispered.

He held his arm out, so calm, used to doing this hundreds of times across the years. "*You're* not doing this. *We* are."

He offered a tentative smile, and I placed my trembling hand on his arm as we fell in line behind our family. The entryway to Chetwin Palace was marked by large, circular stone posts driven into the ground, making an edge for the stone path. Unlike the wide gravel area to leave horses and carriages at Keresken, there was a semicircle drive, and we were expected to disembark while the drivers moved the coaches to another area. It left room for a wide lawn, and, while it was a pretty piece of land, it was simply empty. I turned away from it, my eyes drifting up the pale stone walls.

Perhaps it was because I'd run from Keresken, from Jameson, but walking into another castle felt like trading bracelets for chains. All I could see were the strings attached to favors, the invisible restraints of expectation. Beneath any dances or feast, there was the weight of the throne. Even those nearby had to shoulder it.

So help me, after this, I would put eons and oceans between me and any crown on the continent. Never again.

I watched as the inevitable happened. People saw Uncle Reid and greeted him warmly, happy to see him. They nodded at Mother and Scarlet, and then seemed to take in that they were several members short of their usual party. And then they saw me on Etan's arm. A stranger. There were squints and double takes, though most people were polite enough not to make a comment.

Every once in a while, I'd catch a murmur as we passed, always communicated in hushed tones.

"Who would the Northcotts invite from *Coroa*?" someone asked.

"Seems a dangerous alliance to make right now," another commented.

It wasn't as cruel as it could have been, or maybe even as vicious as I'd expected. Most people seemed more concerned than judgmental, but I still had the distinct feeling I wasn't welcome.

"I suppose training to be queen made you acquainted with such talk?" Etan posed. He was trying to keep his voice light, and I appreciated the effort.

I grinned. "You should have heard what they said when I fell in the river."

He looked down at me quickly in shock. "You fell in . . . Now is not the time, but I expect to hear about that later."

I giggled. "I lost my shoes."

"Your shoes," he said, finally understanding Nora's comment in her letter. He shook his head, smirking. "Unbelievable. Did Silas know about this?"

"Happened before he came, and he mentioned it the first time we spoke. *Everyone* knew about it."

Etan properly laughed then. "Perfect."

I was used to a crowded court, used to the noise and lack of space. It probably should have felt like stepping into a trusty pair of boots, but I couldn't settle. I tried not to hold on to a single sideways glance as we made our way to the throne. The same gray-white stone was everywhere, and the windows were tall and thin, letting in light at long and tall angles. It was nice enough, but it wasn't half so beautiful as the Great Room at Kereskerı. The tapestries were thick but plain, the chandeliers rudimentary compared to Coroa's. It seemed there was no pride in the work, no pushing to see if it could be better.

I was so lost in the plainness of the hall that I didn't see King Quinten until we were coming to bow before the throne.

"Your Majesty," Uncle Reid greeted him, falling low to show his respect. Following suit, fighting every instinct in my body, I curtsied before that monster.

"Lord Northcott," he addressed Uncle Reid, his voice bored. "You seem well. Who is with you?"

"My wife and my son, Etan. Then our relatives, Lady Eastoffe, Scarlet Eastoffe, and my newest niece, Hollis Eastoffe."

At that, a hopeful blonde head peered around Uncle Reid's, and I met eyes with Valentina, seated on her throne. She'd seemed so imposing the first time we met, so determined to leave a mark, good or bad, on anyone who passed her. Now she looked young and scared. She was trying to hide it, of course, as she'd grown accustomed to. Maybe it was seeing the face of a friend that brought her true feelings to the surface. She offered me a small smile, and I couldn't help but smile in return, so happy to finally see her alive and well. She adjusted herself on her throne, so she could keep me in sight, and I just kept staring at her, wishing I could break every rule I'd learned so I could run up and embrace her.

But it didn't take me long to realize that Valentina wasn't the only one staring at me; Quinten was as well.

"Well, well. I'd heard that Jameson had lost his bride, but I didn't think she'd end up in my court. What in the world are you doing here, child?" His voice, even painted in boredom, was menacing, and I had to take a steadying breath before answering.

"I am here with my family, Your Majesty. I am an Eastoffe now."

He sat back in his throne, looking upon us with confusion.

I couldn't tell if he seemed thrown by the fact that I'd married into the family he'd tried to kill, or just that I hadn't been slaughtered along with them. Whatever it was, he looked as unsettled as I felt.

"Are you to tell me you left a king for a *craftsman*? And a traitor to his kingdom, as well?"

"Silas Eastoffe spoke highly of Isolte all his life, Your Majesty. He was pained to leave it." The diplomatic statement didn't even require me to lie. Isolte was close to Silas's heart. The land, the food, the customs . . . it was all still in the very fabric of his soul. The only thing here that drove Silas from his much-beloved home was the man speaking to me.

"Really?" Quinten asked in disbelief. "And if he is so fond of his homeland, why does he not dare to show his face now?"

That beast. He was going to make me say it. I looked around, noting all the curious eyes of his court, waiting for an answer. I willed myself not to cry.

"He's . . ." My voice broke, and I took another breath. Etan's thumb was there, rubbing on my hand where he held my arm aloft. *Not alone*, it said. I tried again. "He is dead, Your Majesty."

Whatever his many weaknesses might be, King Quinten was quite the actor. His brow stayed furrowed as he took in the party of six, noting that there were several members who ought to be there but weren't.

What's more, the room was in shock as they took this in. A few people had silenced themselves as our conversation with the king went on, and now they were tapping those who were still talking on the shoulder, hurriedly whispering the news in their ears. There were only a few isolated murmured conversations happening as Quinten went to speak again.

"And Lady Eastoffe? Is your husband gone as well?"

"Yes, Your Majesty. Him and all three of my boys." Her voice cracked on the last word, but she held herself together beautifully.

He sat there, studying us, and I couldn't tell if he was pleased to see us here, honoring his son as he'd wished, or if he was disappointed to find his work was unfinished. Genuinely, his face was a mask of surprise.

It was such a cruel manipulation that I couldn't look at it anymore. I turned my eyes away, and I caught sight of a man with a short graying beard and a hairline falling into retreat. His lip was trembling as he took in the news. Beside him, a woman was shaking her head as she whispered to her husband in disbelief. I knew Lord Eastoffe to be a good man, and I knew his sons to be followers of his footsteps. Even for people as chilly as the Isoltens, the loss of such fine men was a hard one to take.

"You were right," I whispered to Etan. "No one knew."

He pursed his lips, seeming displeased with this, and, quite suddenly, King Quinten was back to business.

"Widow Eastoffe, I gave your former quarters away when you left for Coroa, as was fitting for your behavior. But the Northcotts' apartments are unchanged, and I think they will suit your number just fine. You may leave us."

I curtsied and looked up at Valentina one last time. She nodded, seeming to want to comfort me with absolutely no way to do so. Etan began to turn, so I followed, switching hands in the process.

Etan quickly led us from the room, only slowing once we were in the hallway. I turned at the heartbreaking sound of Mother weeping behind us.

"It's all right, Mother. No one will call you that, I'm sure," Scarlet said comfortingly. It did little good.

Mother had her head tilted backward at an angle that looked rather painful, resting on Aunt Jovana's shoulder. "*Widow Eastoffe*. I can't bear it. I can't."

"Excuse me? Lady Eastoffe?"

Our eyes traveled to a man rushing from the main room, trying to catch us.

"Lady Eastoffe," he said again, his voice pained, taking her hand. "It can't be true?"

She offered a sad smile to this man. "Lord Odvar. I'm afraid it is."

He shook his head. "The boys, too? Silas?"

She nodded. Before, I might not have noted how he singled Silas out. Now that I knew people once had their hopes tied to him, it made sense. There might still be people who had been waiting for him to return.

Lord Odvar turned to me. "And you? You're young Silas's widow?"

Oh, Mother was right—how that word cut. It labeled you

with loss, taking everything else away. Forget lady, forget bride. I was someone who'd been robbed.

"I am, sir."

He came over and extended his hand. Hesitantly, I offered him mine. He raised it to his lips and kissed it. "I would suppose you were a unique lady if you were truly once on the arm of a king."

I ducked my head. "I was, sir. Once."

"I won't lie. I'm far more compelled to know you as the woman who stole the heart of a man like Silas Eastoffe. Welcome to Isolte."

THIRTEEN

Etan walked decisively down the hallways, which were so snug it was hard for two ladies in their full gowns to walk side by side. They were also much more mazelike than what I was used to, with branches breaking off leading to goodness knows where. I started studying the limited artwork, hoping I'd be able to find my way on my own if I mastered a few landmarks.

My hand still felt warm from where my new and unexpected friend Lord Odvar had taken it. It seemed, even in his death, Silas was making things better for me.

"Just here," Etan said, ushering us all around a corner.

The stewards were already placing trunks inside the rooms, knowing without instruction where we'd be.

"Careful with that one," Uncle Reid instructed as they moved his trunk. It was the last one, and thank goodness, because I needed all the eyes of this castle to disappear for a minute.

The entryway was spacious enough, if dim. I could see that the apartment, instead of going on and on like my last quarters at Kereskin, simply led to four bedrooms.

"You have this one," Aunt Jovana insisted, pointing Mother to what must have been the largest room, their room.

"No, no . . . I won't put you out any more than I already have."

"Then this one," Etan said, moving her to what I assumed was his room.

"Girls, you don't mind sharing, do you?" Uncle Reid asked. Scarlet and I smiled.

"We prefer it," Scarlet answered for us.

"Excellent."

Etan wordlessly claimed the room on the far right of the apartment, so Scarlet led us into the one left of it, and I was pleased to find a large poster bed, several of those thin windows allowing light into the room, and an unlit fireplace against the wall that we shared with Etan.

Scarlet and I went to putting our things away: trunks at the foot of the bed, bags in the corner, dresses hung up to air out. I brought what I had, which was to say dresses more suited to the Coroan court than the Isolten one. But I knew Scarlet would share, and it was only a few days.

"Girls? Etan?" Uncle Reid called. "Come on out when you can."

Etan beat us out into the main room, where Uncle Reid

and Mother had their heads together and Aunt Jovana was smiling at them, seeming to admire their tenacity.

"Ah, here you are," Uncle Reid greeted us. "We've made it through our arrival, and now we need to prepare for the next event: dinner. Tonight, the goal is open ears. Hollis was right that this is probably the best place to find undeniable proof that the king has done something treasonous. Talk to families that live here, see if anyone has heard anything."

He paused, clearing his throat before he went on. "And . . . I think we need to acknowledge a secondary goal. If we're truly endeavoring to topple the crown, and those in this room are the only ones living with any right to take it, then we need to shore up our support. Speak, console, charm. Do what you must. If we prove Quinten to be in the wrong but have misjudged the people's willingness to revolt, then this will all be in vain."

I could tell he was very serious, but this was the least of my worries. If there was anyone who I'd want to rally behind, it was Reid Northcott.

Scarlet pulled my hair up in the typical Isolten fashion, plaiting it into several braids and looping them in a pretty nest on the crown of my head. It felt heavy, but it was a simple way to show my aim was to bend to my hosts' will, and I worried about standing out for Uncle Reid's sake.

"And this will complete everything," she said, lacing blue jewels across my blonde hair, a shade closer to hers and Valentina's than to nearly anyone back in Coroa. The dress was an almost-yellow color, not quite the gold I used to wear, but close enough to feel familiar. The blue was decidedly new.

"Thank you."

"Can I tell you something?" Scarlet asked. "You're the only one I can say it to."

"Of course," I replied, getting up so she could take my place in front of the mirror.

"I remembered something else today," she whispered as she settled. "I remembered there were flames on the curtains before I saw the vase flying. So the fire happened sooner than I thought."

I shook my head. "How do these things come to you?"

She opened her mouth a few different times, trying to begin an explanation and failing. "I don't know. It's like the whole painting of the moment is there, but then I turn my head and focus on one part of it. And when I do? It's vivid and clear. I keep hoping that once it's all put together, I won't think about it so much."

I placed my hands on hers. "I'm still listening, Scarlet. Anytime."

She gave me a tired smile. "I know."

I worked on pulling her hair up, doing something similar to what she'd done for me.

"You don't need to be so nervous," she said, likely noting my unsteady hands as they worked.

"I'm worried people will discount Uncle Reid, given his association with a Coroan who abandoned her country."

"A Coroan who married one of the best men in Isolte, you mean."

I smiled. "He really was. Still, I wonder if I should simply stay away."

"Uncle Reid asked for a united front. You and Etan are doing wonderfully so far, and that speaks volumes for the strength of our family, despite how small it is. And besides, the animosity between our countries is exaggerated. Trust me. It's like when everyone came to visit the Coroan court. Did it seem so bad?"

I squinted, remembering. "No. It wasn't blissful or anything, but it seemed like there were some genuine friendships that reached across the border."

"Because there are. The kings like to talk, and there will always be people who are prejudiced against foreigners. For Quinten, I think it's part of how he maintains power—the illusion that we need someone like him to protect us from someone like you."

I giggled. "I am pretty threatening."

"But you'll see. People who feel like that are in the minority."

I hoped with all my heart that was true. I knew these people existed, but maybe, just maybe, they were dwindling.

I hung my head, suddenly feeling the need to confess. "Would you hate me if I told you I was in that minority once?"

She smiled. "Not at all. Past tense. Done and gone."

I kissed her cheek. "Let's go."

We walked into the main room where everyone was waiting. Mother was pacing. Uncle Reid and Aunt Jovana were talking quietly by the fire, and Etan was lounging in a large chair.

At the sight of us, he sat up a little taller. His usually sullen face transformed for a moment into something that looked almost pleased.

"Oh, girls," Mother said. "You both look lovely." Beside her, Aunt Jovana looked so pleased to see us that her eyes were brimming with happy tears.

"That's everyone. Are we all ready, then?" Uncle Reid asked.

Scarlet and I nodded, and Etan hopped up to come and escort me to the feast.

"You know," he began, "you could almost be mistaken for a lady."

"It's a shame that no amount of velvet could make you look less like a scoundrel."

"A scoundrel?" he replied, testing the word. "I can live with that. Here," he said, offering me his arm, that hint of a smirk still on his face. I took it, falling into our place as the last of the family members to walk out the door.

"Listen," I began quietly, "I know Uncle Reid wants us all together, and Scarlet loves me too much to tell me to stay behind, but I trust you to be honest. If you see I'm getting in the way, say so, and I'll go."

He looked down at me soberly. "I would. You know I

would. But I think Father is right. Quinten tends to moti-
vate by fear; it would be refreshing, I think, to see that
people could be motivated by something else. Hope, kindness, common human decency."

"Wait . . . you possess common human decency?"

"In very small quantities, so I don't use it often," he teased.
And, because it was funny, I laughed. "Just follow our lead,
stay with me, and be as friendly as you can. After that, all
you have to do is eat and dance."

I chuckled. "Ah, finally, something I'm good at."

Etan's smile was wide as we walked into the Great Room,
and I found myself gripping his arm tighter for support. The
thing about a minority of people disliking you was that there
was no way to tell on sight who fell into that minority. So, to
not walk into a situation I'd have no hope of escaping on my
own, I had to act like everyone was in that minority until
proven otherwise.

Our seats were incredibly close to the head tables, which
made sense, as the Northcotts and Eastoffes were the only
blood relatives of Quinten's in the room. The only ones in
the world, as a matter of fact. It left me feeling exposed, and
I wished there was a way to wrap all the fabric dripping from
my arms around me like armor.

"Etan Northcott, is that you?"

He and I both turned to a woman staring across the table
in wide-eyed wonder.

"Lady Dinnsmor, Lord Dinnsmor! It has been too long!"
Etan's face was bright, such as I'd never seen it. He reached

out to take her hand, and she gripped it in both of hers.

"The last we'd heard, you were at the front again. I didn't think we'd see you here," the lady gushed.

"I did go back," he clarified, "but then my father sent for me. I'm sure you will have heard that my uncle, Lord East-offe, and his sons were recently . . . they died. It was my job to fetch my aunt and cousins."

He said this so calmly, linking me in with Scarlet seamlessly.

Their faces said what we already knew: this was news.

"How did they die?" the gentleman asked somberly.

"They were murdered. A raid at my cousin Silas's wedding in Coroa. Allow me to introduce his widow, Hollis Eastoffe."

Their hollow eyes came over to me. "You poor girl. I'm so sorry."

"Thank you, my lady," I replied, taking in her genuinely sympathetic eyes.

"Silas was such a clever one, a peacemaker," she commented.

I thought about that, about how Valentina had once told me that Silas just wanted people to think, how he walked into a swordfight without anyone's colors on, how he never seemed to flinch. No wonder people rallied behind him; he'd been made for peace.

"He was. I count myself lucky to have loved him. And to have gained a new family because of him."

She smiled, looking me over. "So, you're from Coroa, then?"

I swallowed. Minority or majority, minority or majority? "I am."

"And yet you braved coming here with your in-laws?"

"My parents were also killed in the raid. Lady Eastoffe and Scarlet are my only family now."

They didn't seem to be put off by my otherness, only saddened on my behalf. If I hadn't known to look for it, I might not have caught that it happened, but, as sure as the sun rises, they looked to one another . . . and they glanced up at the throne.

"I'm sorry for your loss. It's too much for someone so young," the gentleman said.

"Thank you, sir."

He moved his eyes to Etan. "Do we know?"

"Nothing we can prove."

"Silas," he said, shaking his head. "He hated Silas."

"He did."

The gentleman sighed heavily, almost angrily. "Once you're certain, alert us."

Etan nodded, the Dinnsmors turned to speak to someone else, and we moved so we could take in the rest of the room.

"How do you know them?" I asked quietly.

"I mentioned a Micah on the way here, a friend I lost at the front. Those are his parents."

I looked over at him, gaping.

"They send me things sometimes. Notes and trinkets. A whistle once. I think treating me like a son helps make up for the fact that theirs is gone." His jaw went tight. "It should have been me."

"If you ever say anything like that in my presence again, I will . . . force you to listen to my voice for an hour. I can talk about anything and am very persistent, so watch it."

There was a hesitant smile playing at his cheeks. "I do believe torturing civilians is illegal." He looked at me with those sad eyes.

"Well, you said I wasn't Isolten, so I'm not really worried about obeying laws. Stop talking like that. You're alive. So live."

He nodded, taking one long breath and then focusing his attention back on the room. My eyes went to Valentina. She saw me and barely raised her fingers from the table to give me a wave. I gave a small one back.

"I wish I could talk to her," I murmured.

"Need I remind you that she's the enemy?"

I sighed. "Just when I thought you were getting tolerable. No, she is not."

He squinted at her. "She does look a little pale. Perhaps she is pregnant."

"For her sake, I hope so," I wished, trying to think of a way to get close enough to her to ask. I couldn't just walk up to . . . Etan's eyes were boring into me, stealing my focus. "What?"

"What do you mean by that?"

I swallowed and leaned in so that no one would hear. "She's lost three already. She seemed very nervous about her place when she visited Coroa. I'm worried the king will divorce her if she doesn't . . . what? Why are you looking at me like that?"

"Are you positive about that?" he whispered. "Three miscarriages? You're sure?"

"Yes. She told me herself, but I wasn't supposed to tell anyone. I'm counting on your discretion, Etan. I mean it."

"Have you told anyone else?" he asked.

"Silas. And he wanted to tell his father, but I begged him not to."

Etan shook his head. "He must have loved you tremendously. That is *very* important news. And it explains a lot. Quinten was counting on passing the crown to an heir of his own, and he's never been sure how long Hadrian would live. He's clearly abandoned his hope in Valentina, and now his hope is that Phillipa will conceive quickly. *That's* why this wedding is happening now."

If this was true, all I could think about was poor Valentina, trapped in a loveless marriage to the cruelest king in memory. If he had no hope in her, what would he do? Divorce seemed like the merciful option these days. If he could kill off Silas for standing in his way, what would keep him from doing it to Valentina?

I moved my eyes to Hadrian's bride. I watched her intently, and though she spoke warmly to anyone who came to meet her, when her focus was turned to Hadrian, it was hard to find anything more than indifference in her eyes. Not disdain or sorrow. It seemed more an acceptance of what she must do and of the person who'd come attached to the duty she'd been raised to complete her whole life.

I wasn't sure if I admired her resolve or pitied her. Beyond most of that, I felt a chilling sense of worry. If she failed, too, what would happen to her?

The sound of heavy footsteps pulled my attention away. Six men wearing dirty Isolten uniforms were running into the banquet hall. "Let us pass!" one shouted. "News for His Majesty the King!"

Crowds parted, and the men ran through, all falling to a knee before the head table, one all but collapsing from exhaustion. "Your Majesty, we must report that another battalion has been attacked by the border with Coroa. We are the only ones to survive."

I gasped, covering my mouth in shock. They were all so young.

"No," Etan whispered. "No."

"We came to tell you of this atrocity," the soldier said, "and ask for more men to come with us to defend our land."

"Jameson," Etan muttered under his breath, as if it were a curse.

I swallowed. It was hard to explain my lingering allegiance to Jameson. Perhaps it was because Coroa, for better or worse, would always be my home. I stayed silent, afraid to even attempt to comfort him. Any semblance of peace between us might be gone tonight in that single word.

"I will go and fight!" a man called out from the crowd.

"So shall I!" another cried.

The king shook his head, raising his hand to silence the room. "I will not waste our precious blood for that villain of a prince!" he yelled above the guests. He sank for a moment into his throne, mumbling to himself. Phillipa looked to her fiancé, as if to ask if this sulking was normal, and Valentina sat on the farthest side of her chair as physically possible. Once his anger had finally settled, he called out into the hall. "Where is *that girl*?"

FOURTEEN

THERE WERE SCORES OF PEOPLE in this room, but I knew deep in my bones that he was looking for me. King Quinten confirmed my suspicions as he called out again. "Where's that girl the Widow Eastoffe brought with her?"

It was easy for him to find me, as most people in the room turned to stare at our table and the stranger accompanying the Northcotts.

"Up on a bench, girl, so I can see you!" King Quinten commanded.

"This should be interesting," Etan mused, offering a hand so I could climb up on the seat.

"How can you joke about this?" I hissed.

"This has been my whole life, darling. Welcome to the family."

I trembled, taking his hand and stepping up on shaky legs.

"Yes, there you are. Lady Hollis, Jameson's former bride."

At that, many whispers went up around the room. Like the Dinnsmors, not everyone had heard of me yet.

"I've been told that, despite your many sins, your precious King Jameson wishes for you to return to the palace. I heard he burned half of it down when you left, grief stricken as he was."

Etan looked up at me, waiting for me to explain, as this was the second time we'd heard that rumor.

But there was no explanation. It wasn't true. There *was* a fire, but . . .

King Quinten riffled his fingers through his thin white beard and eyed me like a hawk stalking a mouse.

"Perhaps we should send you back to Coroa in a burial shroud," he commented offhandedly. "Maybe the loss of his precious Hollis would finally teach him some respect."

Murmurs of agreement came up from around the room, and, suddenly, it felt like the minority had vanished. Here, in the moment of their countrymen being killed at the hands of mine, I was the face of the enemy . . . I couldn't imagine any room for mercy.

"I beg your pardon, Your Majesty?" I squeaked out.

"If Jameson so easily kills my people, why should I not do the same to his? Maybe I'll finally have his attention if I take away someone he values instead of his pathetic, worthless soldiers."

Was he trying to scare me? Was this just a joke? Jameson preferred bizarre forms of entertainment, so I couldn't rule out the possibility. Not from the man who took my parents, who took Silas.

"Do you have a better solution?" the king posed to me.

I stood there, struggling to catch a breath. I was going to die, and I'd done nothing to stop this man. I'd failed Silas, my family, and so many others. On top of that, if he did send my corpse to Jameson, he'd probably end up inviting a war into his kingdom, not ending one.

"Say something," Etan urged under his breath.

"Er, Your Majesty? Is it not true that the kingdom of Isolte is more than twice the size of Coroa?" I called out.

"Indeed, it is. With far better land and generous access to the sea."

Across the room, several cheered and shouted out their agreement that Isolte was superior to any country on the continent.

"Then, Your Majesty, would it not be worth consider-ing . . . gifting these scraps of land along the border to King Jameson?" At the mere suggestion, cries of anger arose from the room . . . but it was not as loud as I expected it to be, not nearly as dense. I raised my voice over them, over the minority. "Perhaps the king acts out of jealousy. Considering your many resources, one could understand it," I continued, unsure if my attempts at flattery would work.

"If . . . If you give up these paltry pieces of earth, the size of your kingdom is hardly changed, and King Jameson would then be indebted to you. And! And you would find yourself remembered as a peacemaker in both Coroa's history books

and yours." I swallowed. "Which I'm sure would be a welcome change," I mumbled under my breath. Etan cleared his
throat to cover a chuckle.

A hush fell over the room.

I stood there, waiting for someone to do something. Anything. Break into a laugh, draw a sword. There were too
many possibilities.

"This is an interesting thought," the king finally mused.
"It would be nice to see Jameson groveling."

Some in the room cheered rowdily.

The king waved a hand to his butlers. "See these men
have fresh clothes and food." Then, turning back to the soldiers, he continued. "You will stay the night as my guests,
and I will tend to this dispute in the morning. For now, let
us return to our festivities. My only son is getting married,
and *no one* should disturb such a perfect celebration."

He looked at me as if I'd climbed up on the bench at my
own prompting.

The music began again, and I nearly clawed Etan's ear off
trying to scramble down from my perch.

"Could I please go back to the room now?"

"Certainly," Etan said, his face clearly amused.

"Go fast," I begged.

We exited the hall to an onslaught of attention, which
made everything worse. Once we rounded a corner and the
noise died down, I lunged for a large cistern and vomited.

"Couldn't hold up the lady act all night, could you?" Etan
teased, enjoying this.

"Stop talking."

"I will say I'm impressed you made it out of the room alive, so maybe you've earned the right to throw up all the king's fine food into his personal possessions."

"I mean it. Stop." I slumped down the side of the wall, trying to think of how I would explain the stains on her sleeves to Scarlet. "These are such a nuisance," I lamented, holding up my arm. "I don't know if I can keep wearing these ridiculous things."

Etan came down and wrapped an arm around me, pulling me to my feet. "But you will. For now." His tone was almost gentle. At least for him. "Come on, let's get you to bed."

I was feeling less and less anxious the farther I got from the banquet, but I didn't know how I would manage to stay bright and charming for two more days.

"It will be different tomorrow," Etan said, as if reading my mind. "Everyone's attention will be focused on the tournament."

"Perhaps no one will care, then, if I don't attend."

He laughed. "I wouldn't go that far, but you should be able to stay out of trouble for a day. . . . You *can* stay out of trouble for a day, can't you?"

"I will if you will," I replied groggily.

"Oh, well, it's all out the window, then."

I couldn't bring myself to appreciate his newfound wit at the moment. I just needed to get to my bed.

"That was very brave," Etan finally admitted. "Suggesting he give up the land. It would not be a popular idea, but it would save so many lives if he actually did it. You should be proud of that, Hollis."

"If I survive the trip, I'll try to remember that." I swallowed. "I'm sorry. I'm sure you lost people you knew today."

"I'll have no way of knowing for a few days. Even if I didn't know them, it's still hard to stomach." He looked around the hallway, continuing to support me as we walked. "I know you think I hate everyone, but I don't. My heart bleeds Isolten blue, and the people here only represent the tiniest fraction of the country. There are more out there, barely getting by, living in fear of an angry king, going to protect the border for money to support their families only to die in the process. I can't forgive Jameson for killing our people, and I can't forgive Quinten for killing his own. It's just . . . they don't deserve that."

We moved in silence for a while.

"It makes sense why you would hate me."

He huffed. "I don't *hate* you. I'm just not particularly fond of you."

"But you did hate me. You said so."

"So did you," he reminded me.

"Yes. I think that Hollis—the one back in the manor, who was tired and sad and trying to do the right thing—I think she meant it. But despite how true it felt then, I probably could not say it again now."

"Because I'm so charming?" he joked.

I shook my head, regretting the movement almost instantly. "Because you came after me when I know you didn't want to. And you've kept your word ever since."

We were just at the hallway that led to our apartments when he paused. "And you've kept yours. Also, for some forsaken reason, you make me laugh when little else does."

I looked ahead, thankful to be close to sanctuary. "You only laugh because you like making jokes at my expense."

"True. Very true," he said, escorting me into the rooms. "Still, it's effective."

Acting the gentleman his title implored him to be, he opened the door for me, allowing me a moment to make sure I was steady on my feet before leaving.

"Go and rest," he instructed. "I'm sure Father will want to regroup after the feast, but Scarlet or I will tell you everything if you're still feeling poorly."

"Thank you."

"What does that look mean?" he asked, gesturing at my face.

"Scarlet and I were joking about becoming gypsies, and I'm just wondering if it's too late."

He laughed and reached for the door, heading back to the feast while I moved directly to the bed.

FIFTEEN

"Are you awake?" Scarlet whispered from across the room.

"Barely," I confessed. I cracked my eyes open to see the stars were now out in abundance on the other side of the window. "How was the rest of the feast?"

"Uncle Reid wants to meet and talk about just that. Do you want me to let you sleep?"

"No, no." I hoisted myself up. My stomach had settled, and I wished I had something to eat now. It would certainly help. "I want to know everything that's happening."

Scarlet came over and took my hand, helping me walk. "You poor thing. That had to be terrifying."

I elbowed her. "Better people have gone through worse."

She gave me a small smile, a thing that felt like an absolute gift these days, and we joined the rest of the family.

"Hollis Eastoffe, you clever girl," Uncle Reid greeted me.

"You stayed incredibly calm under pressure back there. I know soldiers who would have broken into tears if His Majesty made any such threat to them. Well done."

Mother was nodding and smiling but looking smug, as if she already knew I had that in me.

"Well, I suppose the maid who finds the cistern full of my sick won't have such a high opinion of me, but I'll take what I can."

Etan laughed, but quickly silenced himself.

"We're all proud of you regardless." Uncle Reid clapped his hands together, looking at each of us in turn. "It seems Etan's suspicions have been more than confirmed; I had countless people come up to me tonight and ask if it was true that Dashiell and the boys were dead. No one knew until today, and they simply couldn't believe it."

"Those who supported Silas as a future king were particularly crushed," Aunt Jovana added. "I still don't understand the secrecy."

"Perhaps he knows he's gone too far this time," Scarlet offered. "It's one thing to threaten a wing of the royal family, and another entirely to attempt to wipe them out."

Uncle Reid shook his head. "It's possible, but there's something missing here. I can't quite say what it is."

"All I know is that we have more friends than I thought," Mother said. "And the Northcott name has more support than ever."

Uncle Reid sighed. "That's encouraging. Truly. But it means nothing if we find no proof. No one will act if they could be imprisoned or worse for being wrong. We have to find evidence. Did anyone have any luck on that front tonight?"

Everyone in the room shook their heads, too disappointed to even speak their failure aloud.

Scarlet sighed. "The best I could manage was getting Lady Halton to have a little more wine than one ought. And all she did was complain about Valentina. They keep going on and on about her not giving them an heir." Scarlet rolled her eyes, not aware of how important this very point of contention was.

Etan looked at me, his eyes pleading with me to share Valentina's secret . . . and suddenly, I knew why I had to.

"This cannot leave this room," I began.

Their attention focused squarely on me.

"Valentina has suffered three miscarriages."

Mother gaped, and Scarlet went wide-eyed.

"Are you certain?" Uncle Reid asked.

"Yes. She told me herself. I know that you don't consider her an ally, but I do. Ever since the tournament in Coroa, we've had an understanding, and she's . . . she's important to me." I swallowed, taking in their questioning eyes. "But I'm starting to think she could be important to all of us."

"In what way?" Aunt Jovana asked.

"In Coroa, we were talking about Jameson and Quinten, comparing their personalities. Somewhere in there, she started opening up. She doesn't keep her distance from people by choice; Quinten insists upon it. He's keeping her isolated.

And she was . . . concerned for her safety. She tried to deny it later, but she knows her place here all depends upon her having another son for Quinten, and she's lost three now.

"If *she's* in danger, and *we're* in danger, maybe she would be willing to help us."

A light flickered behind Uncle Reid's eyes. "Hollis . . . Hollis, of course! She has the best chance of anyone in the palace to get into the king's rooms. She would know the safest paths in and out of his offices, where his papers are kept. If we could guarantee her safety, I bet she'd at least go and search for us."

Etan shook his head, but it wasn't in disagreement or defeat; he looked as if he wished he'd come up with this first.

"I'd just need to speak with her. Alone." I placed my hands across my stomach, the urgency of all this making me feel queasy again. Once more, I wished I had something to eat.

"The tournament's tomorrow," Aunt Jovana said. "She'll certainly be there. There has to be a way to get a note to her in the busy crowd."

"Then that's our plan," Uncle Reid said resolutely. "Hollis, write a note to arrange a meeting with the queen. Tomorrow, we will get you close enough to give it to her. Whatever time you designate to meet, we will try to arrange a distraction." He sighed. "And we'll figure out the rest after that."

"Bravo, Hollis," Scarlet whispered, reaching out to take my hand.

"Save your praise until this is over. Then I expect to be

showered in your unending affection."

She giggled. "Done."

Everyone stood to go to bed, and Mother came over to kiss Scarlet's and my cheek. "My brave girls. Good night, my loves."

We turned, still hand in hand, and Scarlet rested her head on my shoulder.

"Two decent ideas in one day," Etan said. "You must be positively exhausted."

"Too exhausted to argue."

"Thank goodness. Oh! Here." He reached into his pocket and pulled out a piece of bread wrapped in cloth. "I thought that would help your stomach."

I stood for a moment, staring at it.

"Don't worry, I didn't poison it. I was all out."

I smirked and took the bread. "Well, if you were out. Good night."

"Good night. Good night, Scarlet."

She nodded at him, smiling to herself as we headed back to the room. I took tiny bites of the bread while I sat at the small desk, composing a short note for Valentina. I was happy to help my family, but deep in my heart, I just wanted to embrace my friend again. Hopefully, I'd get to do just that tomorrow.

SIXTEEN

"EVERYONE ELSE HAS ALREADY GONE," Scarlet told me, coming back into our room. My resolve had faded with the new day, and I was a bundle of nerves. I still wasn't used to these Isolten dresses, and the fit of the sleeves was taking longer to adjust than I'd hoped. The rest of the family had left to find a good position for communicating with Valentina while Scarlet stayed behind to help me get properly dressed. "Don't worry," she said in what was meant to be a calming voice, "we have plenty of time."

"I know. I'm just so flustered. What if I can't get the note to Valentina? And if I do, what if she can't talk to me? And if she does, what if she won't help us?"

"Then we'll come up with another plan," Scarlet said sternly to my reflection. "Now, this is the last knot, so be still."

I was tied securely into my gown, weighed down in

Isolten sleeves, and as ready to face the crowd as I was ever going to be.

"Don't forget this," Scarlet said, handing me my handkerchief. Sometimes I looked at my possessions from Coroa and had the sensation I was looking at something that belonged to another person in another time. I'd loved my handkerchiefs so much. I'd embroidered my initials into them myself, added the gold trim all on my own.

Swallowing hard, I crammed it up my sleeve, hoping to keep it mostly hidden. I knew it was also customary in Isolte to give out tokens, but I just didn't have the heart for it anymore. With Jameson, it felt like we were snubbing the meanest ladies when he took my favors, and it was a pure thrill when Silas picked my handkerchief from the grounds and wore it. But now? Here? It felt wasteful, foolish. If I didn't have something important to do, I'd have hidden from the whole affair. Besides, who in their right mind was going to take a favor from me?

Scarlet and I marched outside, and I stayed behind her, knowing she was my guide today. On the west side of the castle, a large tournament ground stood. It was bigger than the one at Kuresken and covered in Isolten blue.

I could see the illustrious stand set up for the king, its tapestries billowing in the breeze. Special guests were already sitting in the box, with many others cramming into the areas nearby. I spotted Valentina there, her one lady sitting directly behind her. Uncle Reid was in place, too, diagonal from the king's box, holding on to a perfect position for us to slip a note if the moment arose.

"Lady Scarlet?"

She jumped a little before turning to the voice.

"I'm sorry!" the rider said from his horse, lifting his visor to show embarrassment painting his freckled face. "I didn't mean to startle you."

"Julien?" Scarlet guessed tentatively.

"Yes. I've been wanting to say hello to you, but I haven't been able to catch you on your own. You seemed to be in the heart of a dozen conversations last night, and I didn't want to intrude."

His eyes were bashful, and I could see his posture belonged to someone desperate to get a moment right, but fearful they were getting it wrong.

"That's very thoughtful of you, Julien. It was a bit over-whelming. I'm hoping to simply sit back and enjoy the spectacle today."

"Of course," he said, flustered. "I don't want to keep you. I just wanted to extend my condolences about your father and brothers. And to tell you I'm glad you're back in Isolte. I suppose you're not up for dancing just yet, but the court has looked dull without you."

His freckles disappeared under a blush.

"I believe that," I commented, diverting attention. "Even the ladies in Coroa were envious of what a keen dancer Scarlet is."

Julien gave a quick nod in his helmet. "High praise, indeed. I got to go to Coroa last year for the king's meeting.

It was one of the most entertaining trips of my life."

I returned his smile. "I'm glad."

Seeming unsure of what else to say, he turned his attentions back to Scarlet. "If your family needs anything, please let me know. It sounds like you all came back in a rush, so if you . . . that is, if there's something you didn't bring or . . ."

"Thank you, Julien," she said, saving him from his bumbling.

"And . . . I hate to be a bother, but could you do something for me?"

"I'll try," Scarlet answered hesitantly.

"I've already asked two girls for their favors and was denied. I didn't think you had anyone special at court . . ."

"Oh! No, I don't mind at all." Scarlet pulled off her handkerchief and placed it in Julien's palm. "Here."

I didn't miss that his hand wrapped around hers, holding it just a moment longer than necessary. And while I knew Scarlet was in no place to be courted, she didn't jerk away.

"Thank you, Scarlet. I'll feel a lot better having your token with me. Wish me luck!" He trotted off to join a pool of other young men dressed in metal suits, and I moved Scarlet toward the Northcotts.

"Family friend?" I wagered.

"Yes. We've known the Kahtris our whole lives," she confirmed. "It's been quite some time since I've seen Julien, though."

"He seems nice."

"Yes." She tilted her head, watching him. "I'm glad he has

my handkerchief. Some of the riders get on edge if everyone else has one and they don't."

I pushed mine deeper into my sleeve and sighed. "We'll have to applaud the hardest for him when he rides."

She nodded but said nothing else. I wasn't about to get my hopes up, and I certainly wasn't going to mention this to Mother, but Scarlet had hardly been speaking, hardly been smiling. Anything that gave me a glimmer of the girl who walked into my apartments a few months ago so ready to dance was welcome to me. So I was now Julien Kahtri's biggest supporter.

We walked around the field, waving to Mother, who looked pleased to find us in the crowd.

"Look at all those riders," I said to Scarlet, pointing to the jousters set up under the trees, talking and laughing as they waited for the festivities to begin. "This could go on for most of the day."

"Don't worry," Scarlet began. "I planned on pretending to faint after an hour or so to get out of here anyway. You can come tend me."

"You were going to abandon me? I'm wounded!" I teased.

"I said you could come, too!" she wailed in mock complaint, her eyes glimmering with mischief.

We took our seats next to Mother, Aunt Jovana, and Uncle Reid. I looked over my shoulder and made eye contact briefly with Valentina. She was close enough to call out to, but I couldn't say a word. I had to find a way to approach her.

"Excuse me?" I didn't turn at first because I knew no one

here, but then Scarlet tapped me on the shoulder and pointed me to the trio of girls looking right at me.

"Oh. Um, yes?"

"You're Hollis, right?" the girl in front asked.

"Lady Hollis," Scarlet corrected her.

"Yes, of course," the girl said, her tone almost too sweet. "We were curious . . . we heard that before you married Silas, you were engaged to King Jameson. Is that true?"

I looked between the three of them, trying to understand their curiosity. Majority or minority? Friends or enemies?

"Not exactly. I was never given a ring, but it was close." I shrugged. "It was hard to tell where being his favorite dance partner ended and being his betrothed began . . ." Even this little bit of information felt like I was saying too much. I realized even after all this time, I was still trying to figure out just who I was to Jameson.

I supposed I was his fiancée in a way, even if it never made it onto paper—and thank goodness for that. A shudder went through me as I thought about promises on paper.

"Anyway, I married Silas, found myself a sister," I added, looking over to a hesitantly pleased Scarlet, "and my dearest friend shall soon be queen of Coroa. I hope. I'm very pleased for both her and King Jameson."

One of them shook her head. "So, you gave up being queen?"

"Yes," I confirmed.

"On purpose?"

"Yes. To marry Silas."

The girl in front crossed her arms. "King Quinten was right. All Coroans should be tossed into the sea."

The words were as sharp as a slap across the face, and they left me breathless.

"What?" Scarlet replied sharply.

"Silas was handsome and all, but that's just common stupidity. Who passes up a crown?"

I glared at this girl. "And were you first in line when King Quinten was looking for a new bride?" I snapped quietly.

She swallowed and raised her head, looking at me down her nose.

"You ought to be ashamed of yourself, Leona Marshe!" Mother scolded. "I'm tempted to tell your parents about your disgraceful words."

Leona finally looked away from me, shrugging as she did. "You could try, but I'm confident they'd agree." With that, the three girls walked off, and I was left dazed.

I didn't look around, not wanting to know who had overheard. It was true that in my short time at Chetwin Palace, most of my interactions had been kind, even positive. This one was so cold that it froze all the others from my memory.

"We can leave," Scarlet offered sympathetically.

"I'm not leaving." I stared ahead, looking at the first riders as they set themselves up, refusing to give away just how shaken I was. "We still have a job to do. I can't go anywhere until that's done."

SEVENTEEN

I KNEW THE RULES OF the joust well enough, as it had been Jameson's favorite event. The goal was to land a hit on the other rider's shield as he passed in the opposite direction, and you received even more points if you knocked the man to the ground. There were other rules, too, about the speed of the horse or hitting a helmet, which would take away points as quickly as you'd earned them, but all anyone cared about was watching someone getting hit.

I wasn't particularly fond of the sound of lances hitting armor, and I was still haunted by the three men I'd seen die during the sport, one at Jameson's own hand. But regardless of what happened today, I refused to leave the arena.

I kept looking over my shoulder. I needed to get to Valentina.

"Are you all right?" Uncle Reid asked after a few rounds.

I nodded.

"Good. Here." He handed me his handkerchief. "The queen looks warm."

I supposed in Isolte, this weather could pass for warm. I took a deep breath and snatched up the handkerchief, carefully sliding my note into the folds. I watched Valentina intently as I approached, hoping to convey wordlessly that this was more than a gesture. But first, I went to her husband.

"Your Majesty," I greeted him. King Quinten looked up, realizing I was the one addressing him. I had a difficult time just looking at him, watching him enjoy sport while so many were gone at his hands. Did it not plague him? Did it not keep him awake at night? I took a breath and launched into my practiced lines. "I wanted to take an opportunity to apologize for last night. I was nervous and may have spoken out of turn. I'm very sorry, and I wanted to thank you for welcoming me—and my family—into your home."

He eyed me curiously. "Not a terrible idea about the land," he said, though it was clear the words tasted like vinegar in his mouth. "You're quite attached to being a clever thing, aren't you?"

"I've found it unwise to be attached to anything these days, Your Majesty."

He gave a lone chuckle. "In your case, I couldn't agree more."

My blood started to boil at his casual attitude. I supposed my fractured heart was of little consequence to anyone else in the world, but seeing as he was the cause of it, he could at least have the courtesy of keeping his disgustingly crusty mouth shut about it.

"All the same, I'm talking to my men. I should have been in the Coroan history books long before now. I'm already mentioned in Great Perine's and Catal's. There's still time for more." He waved me away.

I curtsied, thinking and feeling too many things, and then turned to face Valentina. "For your brow, Your Majesty. You look warm."

She took it graciously and I retreated without another word, afraid to look back and see if she found the note.

"Nicely done," Mother said when I got back to our seats.

"I'm shaking."

"It will be fine," she assured me.

"It's not just that . . . it's Quinten." I swallowed, trying to slow my heart. "I don't want to waste my life hating someone, but it's almost like he welcomes it. He'd rather be known for being wicked than never be known at all."

She wrapped an arm around me. "If I have anything to do with it, a day will come when you won't have to remember his name, period. None of us will."

I placed my head on her shoulder for a moment, allowing myself to be held. I had to believe that if Quinten could speak so callously to the victims of his crimes, he had to be careless enough to leave proof somewhere. Somehow, we would find it. We'd find it, the people would rally behind Uncle Reid, and we would make things right for Isolte.

As the tournament went on, I was hardly able to keep up with what was happening in front of me. When the crowd applauded, I joined in. When they gasped, I followed suit. Everything was explosive and quick, and my mind was dizzy simply from trying to sit still and watch.

I'd been too distracted to notice the rider who had stopped just in front of us, and I was thankful that I managed not to scream when I turned to find a lance before my face. When it didn't move, I realized he was waiting for my favor.

"This isn't funny," I mumbled to Scarlet.

"Hollis . . . it's Etan."

I turned, staring through the slits of his visor. I could barely make out his eyes—the same blue-gray that was etched into every stone I passed. Yes, it was absolutely him. And then I realized the enormous kindness he was showing me, the statement he was making to everyone in that crowd. I was welcomed in his family; I was welcomed in Isolte. The Northcotts didn't distrust Coroans. So why should anyone else?

I stood, pulling the handkerchief from my wrist and tying it to the end of his lance.

"Thank you," I said quietly.

He only bowed his head before moving back to the edge of the field.

"Have you ever seen Etan joust before?" I asked Scarlet as I sat back down.

"Many times."

"Is he any good?"

She tilted her head. "He's gotten better."

"That's reassuring," I replied with a roll of my eyes. "If he gets hurt, that's going to look *really* bad."

She rested her head at a slant, looking at the field. "But imagine how spectacular it will look if he does well."

It was another four matches before Etan pulled up to the end of the field. My handkerchief was now tucked into his armor, the fringes of lace and gold just peeking out along the side of his neck. I hoped that, at the very least, he wouldn't somehow have his helmet ripped off or break an arm. Winning wasn't nearly as important as him simply walking away unscathed.

I clutched my hands over my heart as the flag dropped and Etan and his opponent flew toward each other. For something that was usually so jarring, his run felt slow. I could feel the beat of the horse's legs driving into the ground, and every cheer moved like cold honey through my ears. When Etan's lance finally made contact with the shield of the other rider, it sounded like thunder was ripping open the sky. And then, as if it took no effort at all, Etan had knocked his opponent off the back of his horse, sending him to the ground.

He took off his helmet and ran over to make sure the other rider was fine. Once it was clear the grounded competitor was uninjured, screams erupted from the stands, and I think he must have heard mine over all of them. Our eyes met, and he wore an expression of absolute shock. I could not stop cheering.

Several people around us were clapping Uncle Reid on

the back or making comments about how strong Etan was. Even across the field, people's eyes went to the Northcotts. I didn't dare look over my shoulder to see how Quinten was taking in our moment of praise. Even if he was enraged, I couldn't be bothered to care.

This set Etan up for a very exciting day. The riders were eliminated through multiple rounds, and each time he came back to joust, I found myself nearly caving to the desire to bite my nails. My breath caught every time he charged across the field, lance high, posture determined. And round after round, he came out on top, making his way to the finals.

"The other rider is vicious," I commented to Scarlet. "The way he moves is so intense. I don't think the black armor helps."

"Yes, it does make Sir Scanlan look a little forbidding. And he's always been a very formidable opponent. I think Father lost to him a few times ages ago. But Etan . . . I've never seen him do so well."

"Huh. I guess he finally found an outlet for all that pent-up anger." And thank goodness, because I'd had about all I could stand.

"Hmm" was all Scarlet said in reply. Something in the hitched slant of her smile told me she was up to her favorite pastime: watching everything and revealing nothing.

I clutched her hands as Etan and Sir Scanlan pulled up to their marks, holding my breath as the flag dropped. They raced toward one another, lances locked into position, both of them breaking with a sharp snap as they smashed into each other's shields. Both of them split their lances, earning them each a point.

As they took their next run, a knot formed in my stomach as they both split their lances again, leaving the entirety of the competition down to the very last run.

"I think it has been an hour. Do you want to leave now?" Scarlet asked.

"Very funny."

Our eyes were locked on the two riders, knowing this was it. Honestly, I'd started the day just hoping Etan didn't break a limb, but now, knowing there were people seeing this as him being unafraid of Coroa, knowing that there were people prepared to lend their aid to the Northcotts . . . and knowing those three girls from earlier were squirming in their seats, watching him compete with my favor, I wanted him to win.

I was on my feet as he rode, unable to stay down, my fists clenched with hope and my voice already scratchy from hours of very unladylike yelling. Etan's lance made contact with Sir Scanlan's shield . . . and Sir Scanlan's lance glanced off the side of Etan's armor, which remained perfectly intact.

The arena erupted in cheers, and I embraced Scarlet, crying with joy.

My voice was gone from screaming, and my body was aching from tensing up each time he ran. And it was all worth it. Etan had won!

EIGHTEEN

By late afternoon, Mother, Scarlet, Uncle Reid, Aunt Jovana, and I had happily settled beneath the shade of a tree on the outskirts of the field. There was ale and berries and someone walking around delivering the drumsticks of a bird I'd never heard of or tasted before.

It was a decidedly different feel from Coroa. The air wasn't as soft somehow, and every once in a while, the wind would whip up my hair. I still had the sense of otherness about myself, and simple things like the shape of the trees reminded me that this wasn't just another tournament. But the company made up for anything that was lacking, and I found myself unable to stop smiling.

"That was the first time I've ever cared about the outcome of a joust," Scarlet said, tilting her face toward the sun. It was unimaginably pleasant when the wind slowed. "Etan was *so* good today."

"You led me to believe that he wasn't that talented." I nibbled away at my food.

She playfully slapped my arm as Aunt Jovana pretended to be offended. "I just didn't know how much he'd improved," Scarlet said defensively.

"I still can't believe he won." I was perfectly aware it was all Etan's skill, but the whole crowd saw him take my handkerchief, and, vain as it might be, that meant something to me.

"It's his first, as far as I know," Uncle Reid admitted. "I suppose if the Eastoffes and Northcotts were going to step back into the center of court, that was the way to do it. King Quinten was probably unamused by the win, but it speaks well to . . . others."

"What do you know?" Scarlet asked.

He let out a long sigh. "We have not been forgotten. In light of recent events, some have even said they'd act without proof, that this is enough to warrant an arrest at the very least. If the king is now actively killing off family members, what's to protect anyone else? They fear that their best behavior and loyalty won't save them now. It hasn't for you; it barely has for us.

"But, even if we could remove Quinten without evidence, it sets a very questionable standard. If we don't follow the laws that outline how to legally remove a king, then whoever gets the throne next could be tossed out easily. Let's say it's Scarlet."

"Let's not," she shot back.

"If the laws weren't followed this time, they won't be followed the next. So, in all ways, we will show we are fit to rule. Properly."

Uncle Reid's words reminded me of that silly rhyme we used back in Coroa, the one for when we were taught all the laws that we, as citizens, might need to know. *Undo one, and you undo them all.*

I supposed there was truth to that, that stealing was as bad as lying was as bad as killing. However we went about dethroning Quinten, it was rebellion. Uncle Reid was proving that there was room to undo evil without being evil. If nothing else, I admired that.

"Ah! There he is!" Mother said, pointing at the approaching figure in armor.

We all gave Etan a fresh round of applause, and he waved in mock arrogance, tipping his head in exaggerated ways, teasing us as he took in our praise.

"Congratulations, son!" Uncle Reid said as Etan bent down on one knee beside us.

"Thank you, sir. Good day for the Northcotts." He flipped his prize over in his palms. It was a golden feather, made in such a way that there were spaces between the barbs where light could shine through. It was a fine trophy for a job well done, and it was easily the most beautiful piece of craftsmanship I'd seen in Isolte.

"Even if you hadn't won the whole tournament, the first round alone was enough to be proud of," I commented.

Etan let out a low whistle. "I've had a few good runs in my time, but I've never grounded someone. It's true," he said, raising his arms and gesturing to nothing, "I *am* incredibly talented. But I think I owe some of my good luck to you today, Hollis."

I tilted my head. "Thanks to you, my favors currently have a perfect winning streak."

"Really? Then I think this should be yours." Etan held out his prize.

"It's beautiful, but I can't take this. It's your first win. You should have it."

"Wouldn't have won without you, though. So . . ." He held it out to me, his eyes insistent. With how well things had gone, the last thing I wanted to do was argue with Etan over a feather.

"You're a stubborn idiot, but I accept," I sighed. "Thank you."

"Let's have a toast," Uncle Reid said. "To our champion, and to our good luck charm. To Etan and Hollis!"

"To Etan and Hollis," everyone chorused. And I raised my cup quickly, hoping to hide whatever expression it was that dashed across my face.

"Hopefully our good luck carries over to our plans," I said, diverting the topic. "I delivered my letter to the queen."

Etan swallowed his drink hastily, looking at me wide-eyed. "She got it?"

I nodded. "I checked the ground around her seat, and it at least made it off the field with her. We spoke about the necessity for secrecy in Coroa, so I feel confident she understood the importance of the kerchief."

"When did you ask her to meet?" Aunt Jovana asked.

"Tonight. In the Great Room during the celebration banquet."

They all looked at me as if I were mad.

"Sometimes the best way to keep a secret is to put it out in the open."

Etan shook his head, his expression saying he was once again impressed against his will.

"How can we help?" Uncle Reid asked.

"I'm hoping I won't need much help. With everyone in good spirits from the joust and excited for the wedding, I'm imagining this will be a bit of a rowdy night and that no one will notice Valentina slipping off to talk to me."

"Excellent," Uncle Reid commented. "And the rest of us must be prepared to take in more information. Hollis can't carry all of this."

Scarlet nodded fervently, as did Etan. I didn't think I was carrying all of anything. I was just grateful to be of use.

We finished our food and ambled lazily back toward the palace. Etan was walking tall, his hair still stuck to his forehead from the exertions of his day. He had a very satisfied grin slapped across his dirty face, happily holding his helmet beneath his arm.

"Please tell me you intend to bathe before we go to dinner," I teased.

"Please tell me you do as well."

I chuckled.

"Listen," he began, "I had a thought about tonight, but I couldn't say it in front of Father. I know he wouldn't approve."

"What?" I squinted, trying to imagine what Etan would be willing to do in spite of his father.

"If you find yourself unable to get to Valentina at the banquet, if Quinten or anyone else seems to be watching too closely, I can cause a distraction."

"Thank you," I breathed. "That has been my biggest . . . Wait, *cause a distraction* how?"

He shrugged as if it were nothing. "There were a handful of other competitors today who were more than a little bitter about losing to me. It would only take two or three well-placed remarks to get someone to throw a punch my way."

"Etan!"

"I told you, it's only if you've run out of options. I don't want to make a scene, but it's far more important to get Valentina on our side than for me to uphold my reputation, even though I know that's a big concern of Father's right now. If I'm not beside you, I'll be watching. Simply nod at me or something, all right?"

"Very well."

I knew Etan. He was proud. He didn't like people taking

his work or positions or sacrifice lightly. In a way, his reputation was the prize of his life. To see that he would willingly sacrifice it for now to help me . . . I felt like I saw a glimpse of the person Silas had told me about.

In a way, I felt obligated to change his mind, but in another, I was proud to know him.

NINETEEN

I BRUSHED MY HAIR OUT, braiding the front pieces to hold it out of my face the way Delia Grace used to. The moment her name crossed my mind, I wondered what she was doing now. Had she been moved into the queen's apartments? Did she have a gaggle of ladies serving her? Was she happy with her place at Jameson's side?

I hoped she was. She had been through enough; it was time for her to have some level of ease in her life. I wondered if I ought to write her, or maybe respond to Nora. I'd feel so much better if there was a way to know that Delia Grace had something formal with Jameson.

"What are you thinking about?" Scarlet asked. "You get this look on your face sometimes like you've gone back to Coroa in your head."

If my stare didn't give me away, my guilty smile certainly

did. She was far too observant. "I was thinking about those girls today, asking if I was engaged. I remembered how the holy men had to force Jameson to keep my name off the peace treaty with Quinten. If they hadn't . . . I don't think I could have left."

"What? Why not?"

"I think it would have been as good as being married on paper, or at least practically engaged. Those things are all but unbreakable in Coroa." I turned away from the mirror to face her. "I knew a girl whose parents made a marriage contract with another family when she and her intended were two years old. Contracts like that are dated. So once the date rolls around, you're legally married."

"Oh my goodness!" Scarlet gasped.

"I know. This one had set the date for shortly after the lady's eighteenth birthday, but by the time they were of age, neither of them wanted any part of it. If it's in writing like that, the king himself has to nullify the contract. You're essentially already married, so it's like asking for a divorce. It's no small thing."

"Really?"

"I'm afraid so. A contract is akin to vows in Coroa."

"Even if they were children? Even if their parents did it without their knowledge?"

I'd never thought to question it growing up. I'd been so consumed with hope that someone, *anyone*, would be willing to sign themselves into a lifetime with me that I never thought about how it would feel if I didn't want an arrangement at all.

"Yes," I confirmed. "I was in the room the day of the proceedings. Both sets of parents were still very much behind the match, so, even though the couple were both standing there in tears, King Marcellus refused to nullify it. After being by Jameson's side, I have to believe the king had something to gain from it, but I don't know what. It's the only reason they do anything."

Scarlet crossed her arms, looking both angry and sad. "What happened to the couple?"

I smirked. "They're getting their own revenge. They had an actual wedding, of course. No way around it. But she was the last in her family's line, so she's set to inherit all of their land. He's in a similar position. Their parents clearly wanted one line of grandchildren to get it all in the end. But they're refusing to have children."

"Oh . . . Oh!"

I nodded. "Yes. And it's been several years."

"That's determination."

"It is," I said, turning back to the mirror. "Anyway, I was thinking about all that, and about Delia Grace. She had her moments, but she went through *so much*. I'm glad that, after everything, she could be queen. But if my *name* had been on that paper, it would be much more complicated than me simply leaving the castle."

"Do you think Jameson will really marry her?"

I nodded. "If anyone could plot their way to the throne, it's her."

"If it happens, I'd like to go to that party. That's pretty," Scarlet commented about my hair. "Reminds me of how you looked when we met."

"I think I'm going to leave it down. And I think I'm going to wear one of my own dresses. I just want to feel like myself tonight."

She smiled. "I know that feeling. Here," she said, reaching into her trunk, "let's remind everyone you were in line for a throne."

She pulled out a headpiece I'd seen on her before, a fan made of gold and sapphires, and placed it firmly on my head. We both inspected my reflection. "It's going to look pretty with my gold dress," I commented, "but I'd be lying if I said it didn't make me miss the days when I wore that dress with rubies."

She stood behind me, wrapping her arms around my waist. "No one ever wanted to make you choose, Hollis."

"Etan did."

"Well, Etan has taken several blows to the head at tournaments over the years, so ignore him. You can be both, Hollis. You can embrace both."

I inhaled. "That would be nice."

"You have plenty of time to work on it. For now, we have a banquet to attend."

I quickly got into my gown, and Scarlet laced me in. It felt like learning to breathe again, looking at the girl who had swept Jameson off his feet.

I walked confidently into the main room to meet the family, arm in arm with Scarlet.

"Don't you two look lovely?" Aunt Jovana said, placing her hand to her heart. "It's done me so good to have girls around again."

Etan was watching this all unfold as well. The stubble from this afternoon was now gone, and his hair was slightly tamer than usual since he'd cleaned himself after the joust. He was still wearing that air of confidence that came with a big win, and, surprisingly, he was smiling as I approached.

Our family chattered away as everyone pulled at each other's hems and straightened collars. We all needed to look pristine. I shook my head at them, loving them, even in a state of nervousness. And then I turned to Etan.

He wasn't so terrible looking when he smiled. Some might even call him handsome. And it made me calmer somehow, knowing I was walking into that room with someone I could trust.

"You do look lovely," he commented quietly.

I sighed. "And you'll do."

He chuckled, and I slid my fingers into his waiting hand.

TWENTY

ALL EYES WERE ON ME as we entered the Great Room. Rather, all eyes were on my escort.

"Good evening, Etan."

"Nice to see you again, Etan."

"Why, Etan! How well you look tonight."

It was a chorus of compliments raining down on him with every painful step to the front of the room.

He acknowledged them for as long as he could, then retreated by looking at the floor, laughing to himself.

"Never going to marry, my eye," I spat.

"It'd be a shame for me to break so many hearts," he joked.

"It'd be a shame for you to breed," I retorted. He laughed so loud, it seemed like half the room turned to see what was so funny, only to see the hero of the day shaking his head at a girl from Coroa.

As predicted, the mood in the room was light. It was also much noisier in here than it had been the night before, and growing uncomfortably warm. But the musicians were playing, and the courses were spilling from their plates, and so I tried to enjoy the evening while I could.

There was only one small problem.

I had expected that Valentina and I might have to wait a long time to meet, or that more eyes than I could guess might be watching us. What I hadn't expected was the possibility that Valentina might not be there at all.

I scanned the head table several times, thinking maybe she was sitting somewhere new and I'd missed it. Then I searched the room, hoping she was out making rounds. Neither was true.

"Where is she?" Etan whispered. "Do you suppose Quinten got ahold of the note?"

My eyes went to the king, but he wasn't watching us. He was talking across his son to his new soon-to-be daughter-in-law.

"I don't think so. If he did, it was vague and unsigned, so we should be free from danger. I don't know where Valentina might be, though. . . ."

"I apologize," he said quietly. "For misjudging her. I had no idea she was in such an impossible situation."

"How could you have? He keeps her isolated, and she puts on a good face. I think she fears for her life if anyone guesses how unhappy they are."

Etan sighed. "So, she doesn't care for him? At all?"

I shook my head. "I think she fell into the likes of girls who see the crown far clearer than they ever see the man. I can't blame her."

My eyes stayed focused on the room, but I could feel Etan studying me, perhaps wondering where I fell in that description. I thought I'd seen it all clearly at the time, but I couldn't say for sure now. For as much as I missed it, I wondered if it was best if I stopped looking back at Keresken altogether.

"Etan! There you are!" A girl with a sharp nose and high cheekbones approached, dragging another girl behind her. "Have you met my cousin, Valayah? This is her first trip to court, and she was positively thrilled by your performance today."

"Who wasn't?" Etan joked, standing to talk with them.

I rolled my eyes, but no one was looking. I searched the room again; still no Valentina.

"We do hope you'll be spending more time at court," Valayah gushed. "Raisa and I are counting on it."

Almost as if on cue, another young lady popped up over Raisa's shoulder, batting her lashes at Etan. "Are we making sure dear Etan stays at the castle this time? I have to say, it simply hasn't been the same without you."

Where were these ladies yesterday? Where were they before the whispers started and the lances fell? I supposed it didn't matter.

For all his protests, if Etan loved his family at all, he'd get married eventually for the sake of keeping the name. Even if we never proved anything against Quinten, upholding just a single line of the family would be a small victory. And if he was going to do that with anyone, it would need to be an Isolten girl. She'd have to have blood that went back as far as his, and she'd have to be unwavering. And pretty. And intelligent. And able to keep him in line, because goodness knows what would happen to us all if she couldn't.

Two more ladies showed up, and neither of them was Valentina. It was suddenly far too hot in the Great Room. I wordlessly stood and made my way to the hall.

The main entryway of the castle led four ways. First, to the Great Room. Second, to a large stairwell to the rooms where the king and the permanent members of court resided. Third, to the other rooms for guests, such as ourselves. And fourth, to the pathway outside.

The same gravel path lined with large circular posts awaited me with the cool night air. King Quinten must have felt very safe tonight. The only guards I could see were right by the front gates. None walking the grounds, none here watching the entry. It was, in the midst of so much chaos, quite peaceful.

I stood there, arms across my chest, thinking things I wasn't prepared to, asking questions I had no answer for, until a familiar voice brought me back.

"Hollis?"

I turned to see Etan bounding outside, his expression concerned. I eased his worries quickly.

"Well, if it isn't Lord Jouster Supreme, Defeater of Old Men, Master of Large Sticks. To what do I owe the honor?"

Etan rolled his eyes, relaxing. "Ha ha. I noticed you were gone and assumed you might need someone to guide you to an appropriate place to vomit. I'm merely here to help."

I smiled. "Lucky for you, I'm just fine. It was a little too warm is all. You may return to your adoring crowds, if you wish."

He made an exhausted face, stepping closer. "That has to be the most extended vapid giggling I've heard in all my life. It's still ringing in my ears."

"Oh, come now. I've never known a man who didn't enjoy being the center of attention. Even for all his humility, Silas flourished when he found himself in the middle of everything."

Etan tilted his head, allowing that. "Silas and I are different men."

I nodded. "I've noticed."

He looked down at me, eyes focused as if he was trying to ask me something without a single word. His intent gaze was too much for me, and I glanced away, smiling.

"Next time you'll have to do something ridiculous, like drop your lance or ride in circles. They'll leave you alone after that."

He stood there quietly for a moment before tucking his hands behind his back and smiling himself. "I'm afraid that's quite impossible. I'm far too talented, as you can see. I couldn't be foolish if I tried."

I rolled my eyes. "Speaking of looking foolish, I didn't get to thank you. I didn't want to admit it, but I was feeling a bit awkward before you took my favor. I know comforting me wasn't exactly your goal, but you included me in the day, and I appreciate that."

He gave me a playful shrug. "The least I could do for the girl who threw up into the king's vases. Which some people may have heard about, and I *cannot* imagine who started such a rumor."

I chuckled, jokingly pushing his arm. "You don't have to keep that handkerchief, by the way. I can take it back."

"Oh." He looked at the ground, then back to me. "I'm afraid I managed to lose it on the field somewhere. Sorry."

I shook my head. "It's all right. I still have two or three from Coroa, the ones with the gold on them." I turned at the sound of laughter echoing down the hallway. I watched as three sets of couples wandered from the Great Room, moving their celebration away from the crowd.

"Are you going to head back in there?" I asked. "I'd wager half the free women in that room are waiting for you."

He shook his head, looking away. "I already told you how I feel about that."

"It's not so bad. The whole hour I was married was wonderful," I said, smiling longingly.

"How can you do that?" he asked. "How can you look back on something so heartbreaking with a smile?"

"Because . . ." I shrugged. "Even with all the bad, Silas rescued me. I'll never regret that."

"But rescued you for what? You're stuck in a foreign country with a pieced-together family"—he lowered his voice—"who may be in the middle of losing their lives over a battle that might be impossible to win."

"It's not what he saved me *for* . . . it's what he saved me *from*."

He watched as a dozen emotions danced across my face, reminding me of just how perilous it had all been.

"Etan, I was *so close* to being queen. Jameson was teaching me protocol at every turn, and people came to petition me for favors, and I was going to be the mother of the next heir of Coroa. He was going to make me into Valentina," I said, pointing at the castle, eyes stinging as I thought of that possibility being my life. "I don't know how long it would have taken, but I would have become a shell," I sobbed. "I didn't even know I wasn't in love with Jameson until Silas showed up and took me exactly as I was."

"A terrible dresser with no tact who cries too much?"

I laughed through my tears. "Yes!" I patted at my eyes and nose. "I never had to pretend I was anything but myself with him. With Jameson I felt like every second of my life had to be still and perfect, like someone was painting our portrait. With Silas, things were messy . . . but they were good. I really miss him."

"I do, too. Sullivan and Saul, too. My sisters. The friends I lost at the front. I miss them every day. You can miss people and keep living. Sometimes, you have to."

I nodded, reaching up for just a second to touch the rings hanging around my neck. "I told him I would. It feels strange sometimes, though, to do anything without him. I hope he'd still be proud of me. And I hope we win, because I don't know what will happen to me if we don't."

"You mean, besides the obvious possibility of death?"

I laughed. "Yes! Because if I go back to Coroa, there's a fate worse than death waiting for me."

"What do you mean?"

I sighed. I guessed he should know about it all now. "I'll have to go back to the castle. Jameson summoned me, and I turned him down to come here. It's hard to explain, because I *love* Coroa, and I *love* Keresken, but if I go back . . . I'm afraid he'll completely drop Delia Grace. After those rumors we heard at the border, I can't ignore that possibility. If he is doing that to her, which I sincerely hope he isn't, then I'm terrified he'll let her go for me. And, I don't want to be a disloyal subject, but I also don't want to be his betrothed. Not again. I'm afraid being at that castle means being *his*, and I can't . . . I can't . . ."

The tears came again. It felt like a race. If he'd just hurry up and marry Delia Grace, then maybe I'd be fine. But I didn't want his attention or his crown or any of it.

"Hollis, everything will be all right."

"It won't," I promised. "I know you didn't believe me, but I don't want Jameson. At all!"

He frowned at me. "Why can you talk poorly about him

or Coroa, but when I do it, you get so upset?"

I raised my arms and dropped them. "Because Coroa is *mine*! It's mine, so I'm allowed to talk about how horrible the laws are or my king is. When you do it, it stings because that was my home, and it's a part of *me*, and it's like you're saying I'm terrible, too. As if I didn't already know you thought I was terrible."

"You're not . . ." He huffed as I wiped at my tears. "You're not terrible."

"You just made fun of my clothes," I reminded him.

"Yes . . . I'm sorry."

"Like you're such a great dresser."

"Hey!"

"And why do you like it so much here? It's summer, and it's still cold!"

"Hollis."

"You've got to stop being so hard on me. I can't—"

And then I couldn't say anything else because Etan's lips were on mine.

Every inch of my body went warm, tingling at the sensation of an unexpected kiss.

All my tension suddenly melted away under the sweet kisses of Etan Northcott. I'd never been close enough to smell him before, but he had a scent all his own . . . something that reminded me of being outside. He held on to my arms, keeping me in place, but his hands were gentle. And that was miraculous because I'd seen what his hands were capable of. It was all miraculous, actually.

When Etan finally pulled away, he still held me firmly to the earth. There was a crooked smile playing on his lips, and then, instantly, it was gone. Something flickered behind his eyes, as if he couldn't believe what he'd just done.

"I'm sorry," he said quietly. "I didn't know how else to make you stop arguing."

He let me go, still looking confused.

All I could think was that he'd achieved what he'd set out to do; I was left speechless.

But he didn't make a move to leave, looking as if he was waiting for me to say something, anything. So I willed my mind to stop trying to pinpoint exactly what he smelled like and get back to work.

"I . . . I have to go back inside. I have to see if Valentina's arrived."

His eyes went slightly wide, as if he'd forgotten that was the entire point of the evening. "Yes. Yes, of course." He pulled at his shirt, straightening himself up. "You go ahead, and I'll follow in a moment."

And because he looked so very disoriented, I didn't tell him how I felt about that kiss. I didn't say that I could still feel it, or that he left me deliciously bewildered. I didn't tell him that I didn't mind the dizzying sensation of being the center of Etan Northcott's attention.

Instead, I swallowed that down and locked it away. I couldn't think about what I felt or said or even what this could mean, *if* it meant anything at all. Because when I walked back into the Great Room, it was time to work.

"Please, please, please be there," I whispered. "I can't go back outside right now, so please be there."

I looked down the room, through the throngs of celebrating people, and, finally, mercifully, saw Valentina waiting at the head table.

TWENTY-ONE

THE NIGHT WENT ON SLOWLY, and Valentina and I exchanged glances several times. She kept giving quick shakes of her head that were so small no one else would have noticed them. I tracked my family around the room as I waited, slightly anxious on my own. While their positions changed over and over, two things stayed the same.

First, Julien followed Scarlet like a shadow as she spoke to people, looking like he was working up the courage to say hello again but never quite getting there. And second, Etan was surrounded by a constant cloud of ladies, looking as if he was having the time of his life, taking in their admiration and offering no promises in return.

I supposed he really had just been trying to get me to stop talking.

I slowly wrapped my hand around my waist, surprised to

find an aching emptiness of disappointment fluttering in my stomach.

Finally, when a group of dancers came out to perform, Valentina stood and made her way to the window.

She stayed to one side, looking toward the spectacle that I would have been all too quick to bemoan a month ago, and I looked outside, as if I were gazing at the moon.

"I've missed you so much," she began, keeping her goblet in front of her mouth, the same trick she'd used before.

"I've missed you, too. I was so worried when you weren't here earlier. Did someone find us out?"

"No," she hedged. "I may have needed to slip something into my lady-in-waiting's drink. She is always a step behind me here, and I couldn't have made it to you if she'd come. It took longer for her to fall asleep than I expected."

I giggled a little at the madness of it all, and I was pleased to see a tiny smile on her face.

"I'm so sorry about your baby," I said.

The smile disappeared. "It was awful. It always is. I wished over and over that you were here. I've needed a friend, Hollis."

"Have you been completely alone?"

She gave an all but imperceptible nod.

"At least I've had my family. I hate you've had no one."

"Ugh, I don't mean to be so selfish. I'm so sorry about Silas." She sighed. "It's the sad effect of being on my own all the time; I'm all I ever think about."

"Don't be silly. You've been through plenty. And if you

hadn't, I'd still understand. For what it's worth, I think about you, too. All the time."

Tears welled in Valentina's eyes. "I need your help, Hollis. How did you escape Kereseken?"

I didn't dare look at her.

"I didn't exactly. I told Jameson I was leaving. But if you're asking what I think you are . . . I imagine the circumstances would be much more difficult."

I saw out of the corner of my eye that she reached up to touch her temple.

"Are you in danger?" I asked.

"I don't know. But this wedding means he's lost hope in me. And, honestly, I don't think I could take trying again. But I don't know what happens . . . if you know about . . . Silas might have . . ."

"I know about the Darkest Knights, and, yes, I believe they killed him. And I think the king is dispatching them. So, I need your help, my friend. It would be risky, but we could offer you some protection if you can get us what we need."

She sipped her drink. "Which is?"

"Proof. We need to know he's murdered his own people. Some sort of documentation, *anything* that would give the Eastoffes or the Northcotts the right to take the throne."

She laughed. "You will never snatch the throne from that man."

"That man is old, and his son is barely clinging to life. If they can't produce a legitimate heir—"

"What if I could prove something on that front?" she asked.

"What do you mean?"

She was quiet for a minute. "I can get into Quinten's offices. I know where his most important papers are, though I'm not sure what they say. There might not be a trail at all. . . . If there's any chance, I'll get you what I can at the reception tomorrow. But you will have to find a way to get me out of here, Hollis. I cannot stay."

"Done."

"Good. Wear Isolten sleeves tomorrow." With that she began to casually walk around the room.

We'd done it. We'd gotten the only ally we could possibly have to do the one thing that might save our cause. This part of our plan, at least, was accomplished.

I found Mother's eyes and nodded; she and Uncle Reid both shared a look of relief. Scarlet, who had clearly been watching the entire thing, saw my triumphant expression and tipped her head at me. Aunt Jovana would be filled in later.

And Etan . . . Etan was still in the middle of a sea of ladies, each of them presumably dazzled by his words. Between giving them winks and kissing their hands, he looked up at me. I smiled and nodded ever so slightly, and he gave me one of those knowing shakes of his head.

Whatever had happened out in the courtyard, maybe it would just be left there. Inside the castle, we had a king to conquer.

TWENTY-TWO

I LAY IN BED FOR a long time, just running my fingers across my lips. They felt different. *I* felt different.

I tried to pinpoint the moment, because I felt certain there had to be one. When had I gone from wishing Etan would disappear off the face of the planet . . . to wishing he was in the same room with me, teasing me? I wanted that this very second. I wanted him to come and argue with me or challenge me or give me that shake of his head when I'd done something right. And kiss me. I so desperately wanted him to kiss me.

I couldn't find a when. And I couldn't find a how. But it was there, shattering through all my worry and guilt and hope: my heart was beating for Etan Northcott.

How deep this feeling went, I couldn't say, but having feelings at all made me uncomfortable. We'd been speaking about my late husband before the kiss. It felt like a disregard for everything Silas meant to me to let my heart wake up to someone else, especially so soon. Granted, everything between us had happened quickly. We'd run away together only a handful of days after we had met and married two weeks after that. I'd spent more time as Silas's widow than as his beloved. But I didn't want to treat him like he didn't happen.

Because he did. Silas happened, and he really did save me, and part of why I was here now was to make sure he didn't die pointlessly.

I couldn't abandon all of that for a poorly thought-out kiss that I'd done nothing to invite.

I rolled over on my side and cried. Cried because I missed Silas and felt like I was betraying him, cried because I ached to go to Etan. I cried because the number of things I'd been forced to feel in a matter of months was too much for any heart to hold.

"What's wrong?" Scarlet whispered.

I wiped at my eyes, keeping my back to her. I was so afraid she'd see something in my eyes. "Nothing. Just thinking. About everything, I guess."

"I know. It's been a lot."

"I really love you, Scarlet. I don't know what I'd do without you." I reached behind me, hand grasping in the darkness for hers.

She found it and held me. My sister. I felt like I needed to ask for her forgiveness, but if I did, it would mean confessing, and I couldn't do that. Not yet.

"I love you, too. And so does Mother, and Aunt Jovana, and Uncle Reid. And even Etan. He loves you, too."

"I know." I sniffed, wiping at my nose.

She was quiet for a moment. "I don't think you do."

It took a few beats of my heart to understand the full intent of her words.

My eyes widened. I sat up, turning over to look at her. "Scarlet Eastoffe . . . what do you know?"

She sighed, pushing herself up. "I know Etan hasn't really smiled in years, but you make him laugh. I know he doesn't take ladies' favors because he never wants his wins to be shared, but he took yours. I know he doesn't like to admit when he's wrong, but he concedes to you. And I know he has never, *ever* looked at anyone the way he looks at you. Hollis, for a while now he's seemed like he was walking around asleep . . . he's different now that you're here."

"Really?" I breathed.

She nodded. "He lights up for you."

I swallowed. I didn't know if I could rightfully take credit for any positive change in him, but I wanted to. I wanted it all to belong to me.

"Maybe you're right, Scarlet, but it doesn't matter. He has no interest in settling down. He's flirting. Like with the gaggle of girls falling upon him at the feast tonight."

"Do I detect a hint of jealousy?"

"No!" I replied too quickly. "But let's be honest here. He said himself he doesn't want to marry. *And* if he ever did, it would certainly be with a girl from Isolte, not me. *And* if all of that wasn't true, I couldn't be with him anyway."

She frowned at me. "Why not?"

I looked away. "Silas."

She grabbed my arm, forcing me to look at her, her tone almost angry when she spoke. "Do you think Mother held you down in the garden so you could live as if you had died along with him? Do you think we tried to leave you in Coroa so you'd wallow in his death? Have you learned nothing from all that we've told you about our lives?"

I sat there, stunned. She continued.

"You've seen how we work. When one plan went wrong, we made another. When we couldn't do one thing, we found new hopes. When we couldn't stay in Isolte, we made a new home.

"All we do is live. The point has always been to live. I told you I plan to make it to the end of this alive and free, and I meant it. And if something happens to you and to Mother and to everyone else, and I'm the only one left? I'm still going to do that. You're an Eastoffe now, Hollis. You want to know your part in the family? Your role? Your role is to live."

My eyes welled as I thought back to Mother holding me in the dirt in the garden, refusing to let me go back. "Mother said something like that. She said Silas made plans for me, agreements. I was to live."

She nodded. "Of course he did. She knew it, I did, we all did. So, if you're in love, Hollis, go and live that life. It's the only thing he ever wanted for you."

Tears spilled down my cheeks again. "I know. He didn't rescue me from the castle so I'd be miserable. But even if you're comfortable with me moving on, who's to say anyone else is? And . . . honestly, Scarlet, I'm not sure Etan even wants me."

She shrugged. "I think he does. And I think the entire family would rejoice in your happiness. It's been so long since we've had anything to celebrate. We've lost our homes; I lost my father and brothers. Aunt Jovana and Uncle Reid lost their daughters. Both to sickness, not the crown," Scarlet assured me quickly. "Still, no one wants any of us to sit in our misery. If that's the only thing holding you back . . .'"

I wiped away my tears. "No, it's not. I have bigger plans than this, remember? Gypsies. Goats. I'm not giving all that up."

She giggled. "You're ridiculous, Hollis." She gave me a hug, holding me tight. "We should get some sleep. Tomorrow is the day."

I sighed. "Yes. Whatever happens, Scarlet, I'm with you."

"I know."

She settled back in, looking disappointed that I was refusing to simply say I wanted Etan, but he'd been clear, and I knew it wasn't worth attempting. Besides, we had other things, other possibilities laid out before us. They would be coming with the dawn.

TWENTY-THREE

THE NEXT MORNING, I DELAYED in our room for as long as I could, nervous to see Etan today. Was he going to explain himself? Apologize? Ignore the whole thing?

Ignoring it was certainly my plan until he chose to acknowledge it. Scarlet might have her suspicions, but she didn't know there was a kiss. No one did. And that was how it would stay.

"Ready?" Scarlet asked.

I shook my head.

"Don't you worry. Valentina will come through for us, I know it."

I'd almost forgotten about Valentina. I hoisted myself up, trying not to look as nervous as I felt. "Let's go."

In the main room, only Mother was out and waiting. "There you are, girls. Both looking very smart today." She was patting at her hair repeatedly, as if it was somehow falling out of place. It wasn't. "I do feel it's a bit early for a wedding, but I suppose that leaves for a whole day of celebrating. The weather is so nice for it, don't you think?"

Scarlet walked over, placing a hand on hers. "Yes, Mother. It's a lovely day. And it will only get better."

Mother swallowed, but she nodded and smiled quickly after.

"I'm nervous, too," I admitted.

Aunt Jovana came out with Uncle Reid just behind her. "Did someone say they were nervous? Thank goodness. I've been pacing since I woke."

"You paced while you slept, too, and I've got the bruises to prove it," Uncle Reid joked, and she playfully poked his arm. "Who are we missing? Etan?"

As his name was said, he hurriedly stumbled from his room, raking his hand through his hair and using the other to pull at his belt. "I'm here. Sorry. Didn't sleep well."

Oh, good. I wasn't alone.

I didn't meet his eyes. I wasn't quite ready for that.

"We still have time, son. Take a breath." Uncle Reid said. "In fact, everyone take a breath. Straighten yourselves up, and let's get ready to go."

For the first time since we'd set up this little arrangement, I hesitated to go to Etan. But it didn't matter; he came to me.

My heart was positively racing at his nearness. When I could pull my eyes up from the floor, I saw . . . how could I even describe what I saw? The tension that always seemed to rest in his jaw was gone, and the way his eyes were usually settled in an air of worry and suspicion . . . that was gone, too. He was still Etan, and somehow not.

Usually, he turned to face the door, extending his arm in a very official way. But today, he gently held out his hand for me.

"Come on, you wretched hag. We're going to be late," he teased gently.

I smiled, relieved. I could do this.

"Where in the world did you sleep last night? You smell like a barn." I placed my hand on his, reminding myself that any flickers of warmth I felt were all in my head and not in his, and we were off.

As relatives of the king, we were expected to occupy the first few rows of the temple. Etan and I made our way past the scores of people filling the space to capacity, and he nodded kindly at the many people who greeted him.

The sound of the organ in the background was more ominous than romantic, but I supposed that was fitting. There were a few sprays of flowers near the front of the temple, but otherwise the room was plain. Even the windows lacked color. It certainly all fit my mood about the event. This space felt how I'd always imagined Isolte would: damp, dark, and decidedly less inviting than Coroa. But I'd found warmth here, too.

At some cue that I didn't see, the king and queen walked down the aisle. Quinten looked as venomous as ever, hiking up the aisle with his elaborate cane, and Valentina's eyes were dancing around the room, looking for what, I couldn't guess. Her one hand was resting on Quinten's, and the other was settled across her waist, as if she was trying to convince people that she was with child. They walked on, looking perfectly regal, settling into two thrones on the front right-hand side of the room.

Shortly after, Prince Hadrian and Princess Phillipa entered, walking hand in hand. At that, we rose, and it was difficult to see the procession until they were very close to the front.

Poor Prince Hadrian had a layer of sweat across his forehead already, exhausted from the trip across the temple. His pallor was only heightened by the sight of Princess Phillipa, all rosy cheeks and fair skin.

"This is another concern," Etan whispered to me. "Her father is dead, so her older brother is king, yet he didn't feel obligated to come and give her away himself. He didn't even send a noble to act in his stead. What does that mean?"

"It could mean that this event doesn't matter to them. But I can't imagine why. They're marrying into the largest country on the continent, and that offers unparalleled security. None of this wedding makes sense. The pace, the events around it . . . none of it."

He inhaled deeply, as if he were calculating, trying to make sense of the information in front of him. His expression didn't give anything away if he'd figured something out.

"Please sit," the priest said, his expression serene. "Today we unite not only two souls, but two kingdoms. In the scope of eternity, it is hard to say which of these is more precious. It gives us all a moment to reflect upon our own lives, upon our own small kingdoms, the ones we build around ourselves."

My hands had been up by my chest since we'd taken our seats, fiddling anxiously with my rings. But these words broke through my worry, and I moved them down, holding on to the edge of the pew.

"It is a wise and valuable thing to build up your kingdom, to make walls and leave a legacy that will follow beyond you. It is worthy to make, to grow, to establish. It is the reason so many reach for greatness, the reason so many aspire for glory. We all want our very small kingdom to have a name; we want it to be remembered."

He looked around the room, finally resting his eyes on Hadrian. I don't know what he saw in his face, but he frowned and spoke much faster when he started again.

"But possibly more important than that are the other little kingdoms around yours, the ones you have an opportunity to join with. There is also value in this, in partnering, in coupling. Because what is the point of a kingdom, big or small, if it is enjoyed alone? What value is a castle that only one man walks through?"

Etan's hands came off his lap, also wrapping around the edge of the pew, his right hand resting up against my left, so that I felt the warmth of it—maybe even, I thought, his steady pulse. Was this touch intentional?

"And so, let us pray and bless the union of Prince Hadrian and Princess Phillipa, of two souls and two kingdoms."

Perhaps because of the descending slump of Hadrian's shoulders, the holy man gave a markedly short exchanging of vows, singing through his prayers at such a speed it was hard to follow along. And then, quite suddenly, they were man and wife, prince and princess, the next key in a secure line of succession for King Quinten.

We all applauded as we knew we must, but I felt a part of myself sink. After knowing all that Quinten took from me, it was painful to see him get anything he wanted.

While the king, queen, their son, and their brand-new daughter-in-law filed down the aisle, we stood and waited. As soon as they were out of the temple, we paraded out behind them. At the door, the royal family waited to receive us, to be congratulated by the entire temple of guests before celebrating.

Uncle Reid and Aunt Jovana were first in line, and they bowed and curtsied, keeping everything—their anger, their disappointment, their sorrow—locked up tight. When I got to the royal family, King Quinten was first in line, followed by the new couple, and Valentina was at the end. I was confused as to why Quinten wouldn't keep his wife beside him, but after a quick moment of thought, it made perfect sense: they were ordered by rank, if only in his eyes.

"Congratulations, Your Majesty. Such a privilege," I said.

"I'm sure."

He didn't even look at me but passed me on to Prince Hadrian.

"Your Royal Highness. May you and your new wife have many happy years together."

I realized then that I'd never heard Hadrian speak. I assumed he could talk, but he simply never spoke in my presence. Today was no exception. He nodded, pressing his lips into something that looked similar to a smile, while Phillipa did the talking.

"How very kind. I hear you are close to the royal family. I do hope we'll see more of you at court."

"Perhaps, Highness. That is entirely dependent upon my mother," I hedged, unsure if I could trust the princess, and moved on to Valentina.

She held out her hand as if she expected it to be kissed. When I reached to take it, she gripped my fingers tight and pulled me closer.

"Take these to your room immediately and hide them. Get through the reception. Do not forget me."

From the sleeve of the arm she'd been holding against her stomach, she pulled out several papers and shoved them up the wide sleeve of my gown. I put a hand over it to hold them all in place before sinking into an appropriate curtsy.

Ahead of me, Etan waited with his hand out for me.

"Not this time. I need to go by the room. I'll meet you at the reception." I went with the growing crowd back into the castle, finding Scarlet.

"I need the key to your trunk," I murmured.

Without a single question, she slipped it out of her pocket and into mine, and I broke from everyone once we were inside, heading down the hall to our room. Once the door was shut, I pulled the packet of letters out of my sleeve. I stood for a moment in awe of Valentina. Not only had she managed to get ahold of the information we needed, she'd hidden it as she stood arm in arm with the person she took it from.

I was aching to look through it all, discover just what we had, but she told me to go to the reception, and so I would. She was right, of course; we had to be visible.

Scarlet's trunk was old, and it took several attempts to get the key in properly. When I finally did, I buried the letters, wrapped in a set of stockings, at the very bottom before locking it again. And then, as if it would somehow be safer, I shoved it under the bed.

I took a deep breath and straightened my gown. It was time to celebrate a wedding.

TWENTY-FOUR

THE GREAT ROOM HAD BEEN made over for the reception. Everything was decked in white. Tapestries, flowers, ribbons, the whole lot was clean and clear and pure. The tables were arranged again for dancing, and the newly wedded couple were already sitting at the head table, nodding at those who looked their way.

"Feeling better, Hollis?" Mother asked pointedly. I didn't know who was watching, but I played along.

"Yes. I was bit warm back at the temple, but I'm much better now."

"Have something to drink," Etan insisted, standing so I could take his seat.

"Thank you."

"I am going to eat sweets until I'm sick," Scarlet declared.

"Excellent plan." I turned to survey the festivities. For the first time, I stopped taking in the room as a whole and saw it was very easy to break the crowd down into two sets of people: those who were smiling and those who weren't.

There were some who politely forced a happy face when someone approached them, but more often than not, it looked like people were not as delighted as they were expected to be with this arrangement.

Were people now balancing on a tipping point with Silas killed at Quinten's orders? If we could show them proof, would the majority of this room rally behind Uncle Reid?

I thought of the trunk under my bed, aching to know what those letters said, hoping more than I could say that something was finally falling in our favor.

Etan bent down to my ear, his breath tickling me as he spoke. "Did Valentina deliver?"

He hadn't said anything about last night, hadn't said he wanted to kiss me again, hadn't said he regretted the entire thing. All I knew was that him being this close to me made my skin wake up, hoping that he might touch me. I knew I'd already committed his scent to memory, deciding over-night that if the wind had a smell, it was embedded in him. I knew that if he pulled me into a corner and kissed me now, I'd welcome it.

I simply nodded, and he smiled as he stood back up.

The music changed, and I saw the space in the middle of the floor clear.

"Oh, Hollis," Uncle Reid called. "Could you please accompany Etan in the first dance?"

"What?"

"It's tradition," Aunt Jovana added. "The highest families dance to honor the new couple."

"But I don't know the dance," I squeaked out in fear. "Why not have Scar—" Where had Scarlet gone? I scanned the room, and saw she was holding something that looked delicious in her hands and right across from her was a very tall and bashful-looking Julien, smiling as he tried to talk around whatever he'd just taken a bite of. They looked so precious. Even if I could have raced across the room to steal her away, I wouldn't have.

I turned back to Etan.

"Are you doubting my ability to lead?" he asked, that joking tone ever on his lips.

His lips.

"The only other partners I've seen you with are those fellows in the joust, and I'd rather leave this room standing on my own two feet, if you don't mind."

Mother laughed at that, but Etan held out his hand, undeterred. I took it, and he led me onto the dance floor. "It's simply a volta. If you know that, then you're fine."

"Oh! I love the volta."

"Perfect. Then you don't need me at all."

I looked at him out of the side of my eyes. "You say that as if I ever have."

He smiled.

Other couples were flooding the floor, and I stood toward the center beside the other women, with the men on the outside forming a shape like a flower. When the music began, Etan and I wove past one another, circling around and going to the next couple. The dance was so full of movement that it excused any lack of conversation. So, instead, we danced, hand to hand.

Etan did as he said, waiting exactly where he said he would, exactly when he was meant to. His hair kept flopping in his face, and he kept flicking it back, keeping his eyes on me. I was smiling. I could feel it in the very soles of my feet my smile went so deep. We came to the section where we could move side by side, and Etan held me tight.

He looked down at me, eyes locked. There was something in them that said he wanted to speak, to say something now that all our family wasn't right over our shoulders. He just kept studying my face, maybe trying to judge how he'd be received if he did speak. I tried to wordlessly tell him that I welcomed his apology or explanation or whatever he felt he needed to say. I was prepared for it all.

All he did was smile.

The end of the dance was coming, and it was a good thing, as I was already breathless. Three lifts back to back, and then it would be over. I swept around the circle a final time, coming to Etan's ready arms, and he was smirking, ready to prove he was capable. I jumped as he lifted me up, throwing my head back in delight. The watching crowds were gasping at the sight of the couples moving in time, many of the members applauding. He lifted me a second time, and I laughed at Etan's mocking groan, as if I were too heavy to pick up more than once. The third lift, I found myself looking down at him, and he seemed . . . happy.

I thought about the day we'd met. He must have been so miserable, forced to bring his family into the den of his enemy, into the home of people who'd killed his friends. I thought of how he'd hated it when I'd wormed my way into his home, infiltrating the one place in the world that ought to have been his. I thought of how much anger had passed between us. Where had it all gone? Now he was holding me in the air with such care, I knew if the ground shook the very foundations of this castle, he would still keep me aloft.

People were not their introductions. They were not their lineage or country. They were but themselves. And we had to dig past all the rest to find them.

We finished the dance with a flourish to the applause of the entire room, including the newlyweds. Etan was still holding my hand as he led me away from the floor.

"I haven't danced like that in ages," I said breathlessly. "I didn't realize how much I missed it."

"You're telling me Scarlet hasn't attempted to lift you yet?" he asked in mock disbelief.

"There hasn't really been an opportunity."

"Ah, well." He led me over to a window, and we watched as more couples took to the floor, dancing to something a little bit slower.

"Thank you," I said.

"For what?" he asked.

"I'm not sure. Maybe everything."

He chuckled. "Well, you're welcome, then." After a long sigh that was still tinted with his smile, he added, "And I'm sorry. For last night. Not sure what came over me."

I'd been getting into the habit of kissing boys when I oughtn't.

"Well, it stopped an argument, so bravo. And there's no need to apologize. It's been a very . . . eventful trip."

"And it's not even over."

I shook my head, wide-eyed. "Not even close."

"I'm dying to know what Valentina managed to get ahold of. I suspect Father will read them first."

"We need to find a way to get her out of the castle. I promised her as much."

He nodded. "If need be, I can take her to the country myself. If we don't succeed, the king will never let her rest. If he can find her, he'll make her pay for leaving."

"Then we have to make sure he can't."

Etan looked at me, all traces of his smile gone. "You have my word."

And that was more than enough. "Thank you."

"So, I have a proposition, Hollis."

"Oh, I'm dying to hear this." I propped myself up on the windowsill by my elbow, staring at him intently. Did his eyes always have specks of silver in them?

"After everything, all we've said and done, do you think we could end this, not as unwilling partners in crime, but friends?" he asked hopefully.

If he had proposed this back in Coroa, or even at Pearfield,

I would have leaped from my chair in joy. Now? Now it felt like a lance knocking me from my horse. But Etan and I had very different paths, very different goals.

With a pained heart that reminded me with every beat that this was all we could ever be, I smiled. "I have always wanted to be your friend, Etan."

"Good. Now, one more dance I think," he said quickly, pulling me back onto the floor. "Let's leave them scandalized, Hollis. These poor people need something to talk about."

And I laughed, moving eagerly, remembering the way his hand felt in mine.

TWENTY-FIVE

I WAITED IN UNPARALLELED WORRY as Uncle Reid sorted through the letters. For the first time, I saw Scarlet pray. I knew a little about her faith through Silas, through the vows he insisted we speak, through the traditions that seemed to focus more on people than paper. I'd never been what someone might call pious, and I wasn't even sure if I knew how to pray. If I had, I'd have attempted it long before now.

Still, I folded my hands together and said the only thing I could think of. "Please." It wasn't much, but I couldn't have said anything with deeper sincerity. I sat, head and heart bent down in desperation. "Please."

A moment later, Uncle Reid emerged from his room, a score of opened letters in his hand. We all sprang to our feet in anticipation.

"Hollis, do you know if Valentina read any of these before she gave them to you?"

"No, sir, I don't."

He sighed and set them on the table before us. "Let's hope not. No one should have to read how much their husband is paying to kill their families."

I gasped. "That's in there?"

He nodded. I knew he wanted proof; we all did. It was another thing entirely to have to go through all the details.

"Some of these are inconsequential, but several of them put the king's hand on many of the prominent deaths caused by the so-called Darkest Knights in recent memory, including Valentina's parents. We have names of victims, and I think identities of at least two of the murderers. If this is what Valentina could grab and hide in a matter of moments, there must be so much more."

His heart was undeniably heavy. And so was mine. There was one question I needed to ask, had to. Yet I couldn't find a way to form the words.

But Mother did. "Is Dashiell in there? My boys?"

Uncle Reid shook his head. "There are plenty of deaths not accounted for. That doesn't mean he's innocent in them. But the deaths are not the most shocking piece of evidence here," he said tiredly.

"What could possibly be worse?" Etan asked.

Uncle Reid slowly reached into the pile and held up a single letter. "We wondered why this wedding was so public. It was to mark time. So that the kingdom could presume Phillipa conceived tonight.

"In reality, the king has paid her handsomely to join the royal family. And he has also given a fortune to a peasant girl for her child, one that appears to have been conceived about a month ago."

"No," Scarlet whispered.

Uncle Reid nodded. "He's so desperate to keep his crown that he pushed Queen Vera all her life for more children. And he's pushed Hadrian year after year though it was clear he was never healthy enough to do the job. The only reason that poor boy has survived this long is because of our advances in medicine. If he'd been born in Mooreland or Catal, he'd be dead."

I watched as he swallowed, maybe seeing Hadrian for the first time the same way I saw Valentina: just a piece in someone else's game. "When he worried that our families were stronger than him, he picked away at us. Took our lands, rejoiced when we lost our children, ran us from the country. He married Valentina for her youth. When her parents questioned the king's motives, they were murdered. When she was found unable to make him a better heir, he bypassed her for Phillipa, who is at least smart enough to know who her in-laws are. She wanted money and the promise that once a proper time of mourning passes after Hadrian inevitably dies, she could marry whoever she pleases. She has all of these things in writing," he said, pointing to the letter, and shaking his head. "If Hadrian dies, it doesn't matter. People could still believe Phillipa was having his child."

I couldn't stop the shiver running through me. Quinten had been so malicious, so calculating. He'd played every piece on the board to ensure that he'd never lose his crown, that he'd control who it went to.

"We have undeniable proof now, Father. What do we do?" Etan asked.

Uncle Reid paused for a long time. Then he stood and walked back into his room. When he came out, he was holding a sheathed sword.

"Is that . . . ?" Mother asked, leaving the question hanging.

Uncle Reid nodded. "Jedreck's sword. It has seen war, and it has knighted several men. This is the sword of a king, and now we'll use it to lead a battle."

I waited for Uncle Reid to move for the door, to take some sort of action . . . but he walked over and held the sword out to his son.

Etan's eyes flickered over to me and then back to his father. He was hesitating, and I was stunned.

When I thought of people who would take the throne, the obvious choices were Scarlet and Uncle Reid. Mother was not a direct descendant, and Etan was still his father's son. But, now that I thought about it—why had people been championing Silas instead of his father? I supposed after someone as old as Quinten, they wanted a ruler who still had a lifetime to dedicate to making things right. Etan certainly had that.

"You haven't asked my cousin if she wants it," Etan

offered. "I'd bend my knee to Queen Scarlet." He looked to her, his eyes almost pleading.

I turned to watch her, realizing history was happening before my eyes. She smiled sweetly, taking careful steps toward Etan.

"No," Scarlet insisted quietly. "I don't want a sword, or a battle, or a crown. All I've ever wanted was a chance at a life I could call my own, and I know I'd never have it as queen."

"Are you sure?" Mother asked carefully.

"I am. I've had plenty of time to think about this. I don't want the power or the obligation. And I will *never* challenge you for your crown, Etan. You will have my absolute allegiance, I swear."

Etan's eyes flashed over to me again, then back to his father. "I don't . . . I can't . . ."

"Etan, we've come all this way," his father reminded him.

"Why not you?" he questioned.

Uncle Reid's face was perfectly calm. "If I were younger, maybe. But I cannot lead. Not like you could."

"You are so brave, son," Aunt Jovana said.

"And intelligent," Scarlet added.

"You have impressive military experience, and . . . a *presence* not many people could pull off," Mother agreed.

"You're a natural leader, Etan," I said, fearing I may say too much. Still, I kept on, knowing that now, more than ever, he needed to hear it. "You're passionate, strong, and kinder than you'd let anyone know." His eyes moved to his family and back to me. "Whatever you may think, part of my heart is Isolten, and I, for one, would rejoice to have you as my king." He stared deep into my eyes for a very long time. I watched as fear and hope and desperation flashed across his face. And then, as if the act was almost physically painful, he reached out and took his father's sword.

"What do I do?" he asked.

"Go back to our lands," Uncle Reid commanded. "Call up the army. Take some of these letters with you, and our people will rally behind the truth. We will quietly get word to some of the less-than-happy nobles and explain what's happening, offer them secure places in your government for their support. By the time you get back, everything will be in place. And while I'm confident we have numbers on our side, you must be careful. If you speak to the wrong person . . ."

Etan nodded. "I know."

"You should go now," Uncle Reid insisted. "We will be watching for your return."

"Wait," Etan said, raising a hand. "We need to get Valentina here first." He looked at me. "If she's going to have a chance at escape, I have to take her with me now. I can do that, but I need your help."

I didn't hesitate. "Anything."

TWENTY-SIX

It took a while to find a maid willing to go to the queen's rooms and deliver a message. Poor Valentina. Even the staff feared being near her. Finally, we were able to send word to her that the girl from Coroa had found something of hers and would like to return it to her.

Valentina showed up to our rooms wearing her night-gown and a robe embroidered with silver thread.

"Your Majesty," Uncle Reid greeted her, bowing his head. "We apologize for giving you no warning, but if you're truly ready to flee, this is your only way."

She looked to me. "Hollis?"

I walked over to her, gripping her hands. "Valentina, you have delivered your country. You've saved so many people today. And we cannot thank you enough."

Her eyes welled. "I wasn't sure . . . but it's enough?"

I nodded.

She closed her eyes, letting the tears run down quietly. "Who's to take his place?"

I cast my eyes to Etan.

She turned to him, exchanging a long look. She was about to throw away a crown; he was about to take one. Their circumstances were about to reverse forever, and they had this strange and almost beautiful moment of connection.

"You shall have my endless support, sir."

He nodded to her, his head still going respectfully low.

"Trade robes with me," I insisted, grabbing mine and shoving it into her hands. "In a few minutes, you will leave with Etan on horseback, under the guise of him escorting his cousin home. He will take you to Pearfield, and from there, he'll make arrangements to get you to Coroa. These papers," I said, holding up a handful of parchment, "are to get you across the border, and instructions for my household staff. Hester will guard you. And we have gold." I set it all on the desk beside her.

She stared at the papers, taking it all in. "If he figures this out, you'll be dead, Hollis. I just . . . you have to know that before I leave." Despite her warning, Valentina pulled off her robe and shrugged into mine, her face painted with fear.

"I already know. And I'm choosing to do it all the same. I have very few people left in this world who I care about. You're one of them. I'll take care of you."

Her eyes welled. She looked around to the warm faces in the room. I wondered how long it had been since she'd been treated with kindness. "How can I ever thank you all?"

"It is we who are indebted," Uncle Reid insisted. "In fact, we're hoping you'll be able to forgive us. We should have seen you needed help, and we didn't. We'd have still considered you aligned with Quinten had it not been for Hollis."

Her teary eyes turned to mine. Perhaps there were things we should have said then, words of gratitude or of love, but in the end I couldn't say any of it. I wouldn't tell her goodbye in any form; it felt too final. And if I had to will Valentina into being beside me at the end of this, then that was what I'd do.

"Please send word once you're at Varinger Hall. I just need to know when you're safe."

She squinted at me. "Won't you be coming there soon?"

Etan was looking at the ground just then, and thank goodness. If I saw those slate-blue eyes with their secret streaks of silver, I might have lost any resolve and several pieces of my heart. He was stealing it, bit by bit, with traces of smiles and quiet glances. And what would happen to me when he'd gotten all my heart, and I had none of his?

"Yes, of course. I'll come. I just don't know when. Stay safe," I said, coming over to kiss her cheek.

"We should go," Etan said.

I stepped away, a chill running down my back that had nothing to do with the constant Isolten winds.

"Good luck, son," Uncle Reid said, placing a hand on Etan's shoulder, passing him some of the more incriminating letters. "We'll be waiting for you."

Etan nodded, shaking his father's hand. We had hope that people would follow, but if Etan failed . . .

We'd have no way of knowing until it was far too late.

Etan embraced his mother and whispered something in her ear. I watched as she squinted, taking in the seriousness of his request. He stepped back and looked into her eyes. There was something deeper than a goodbye happening there, almost as if they were making promises. He took a deep breath, and she slowly nodded.

He then moved to Mother, kissing her cheek. "Keep this lot together," he instructed teasingly. She smiled as he moved to Scarlet.

"Last chance to be queen. I'd hand it over in a heartbeat. Without question or remorse."

Scarlet smiled, perfectly composed, and sank into the deepest curtsy.

"Fair enough," Etan said when she stood. He kissed her forehead and moved over to me.

Face-to-face, knowing the danger in front of us, there were so many things I wanted to say. Even if we hadn't had an audience, I couldn't have gotten it all out.

"I *will* be back," he whispered. "Please, *please* . . . stay safe."

"You, too," I breathed.

He laced his fingers through the hair at the nape of my neck and kissed my forehead, staying there maybe just a moment too long, then turned to Valentina.

"Come, Your Majesty; we don't have much time."

Valentina looked at us all one last time and disappeared quietly into the hallway. Etan didn't look back, and I hoped that the flash of his riding cape around the edge of the door wasn't the last I'd ever see of him.

TWENTY-SEVEN

None of us slept that night. And we all stayed awake through the following day. I had no idea how long it took to raise an army, but I would not be able to settle until I saw a pair of gray-blue eyes riding back up to the castle.

I doubted any of us would. Uncle Reid was stealthy but speedy in his work. Unwilling to leave anything in writing in case something should fail, he was in and out of the apartments, passing information to other nobles and double-checking the strength of our numbers.

Even Mother and Aunt Jovana had been receiving guests, the wives and daughters of exclusive families, confirming that they were behind us, and helping those who should have gone home by now provide valid excuses to the staff for needing more time in their rooms.

I didn't know these people, and while I wasn't unwelcome, I didn't feel comfortable adding to the conversation. I wouldn't feel at ease until Etan was back, until it was all settled and done. Before then, anything could happen.

As I was perched at the window, watching the horizon as the sun went down, I whispered my worries to Scarlet as she came to settle beside me.

"He's not hurt, is he?" I asked.

"No, he's not hurt," Scarlet assured me.

I swallowed, sweeping my eyes across the field again. I heard someone snoring. Uncle Reid was deep in prayer, but I thought Mother had fallen asleep in a chair. I didn't look back to check on Aunt Jovana. "No one's accused him of being a traitor and murdered him somewhere in the countryside and left him in an unmarked grave, right?"

Scarlet narrowed her eyes and turned to me. "That's very specific, Hollis."

"It's the image that keeps coming to me. That he tries and tries to explain the truth, but no one believes him. And he's one man against many. I'm terrified he's dead somewhere, and we have no way of knowing."

"Have some faith, Hollis." I tore my eyes from the horizon to look at my sister, and she placed a hand on my shoulder as she went on. "Etan . . . he's *strong*. Maybe too strong. And he's fighting for something good; he won't be taken down. Besides . . ."

She closed her lips tight like maybe she was saying too

much. But she glanced around at the otherwise engaged members of our family and lowered her voice to a whisper all the same.

"Besides, he's definitely coming back for you."

"Shhhh!" I insisted, checking that no one was listening. "We've been over this."

"Yes, and you clearly weren't listening to me."

"I told you. He doesn't care for me like you think he does." I sat up straighter. "He asked if we could finally call ourselves friends. *Friends*, Scarlet. No declaration of undying love, no request for me to wait while he avenges his family, no anything of the sort. Friends."

She let her chin settle into her arms as they rested on the stone sill of the widow. "And why do you think he made such a request, dear sister?"

Because it was the only way to save face after making the massive mistake of kissing me, I thought.

"Because, at the very least, he doesn't hate me anymore, and he wanted to let me know that before we inevitably part ways," I said.

She smiled at me like I was the simplest creature she'd ever met.

"Because he thinks you'd reject him if he dared to ask for more."

I sighed. "And all this time I thought you were so observant." I turned my eyes back to the gate.

"Would you have?"

"Have what?"

"Rejected him?"

"What do you mean?"

She huffed. "If Etan had declared his undying love, if he had asked you to wait for him . . ."

"Oh. That's . . . He didn't ask that."

"For goodness' sake, but if he *had*, Hollis."

"No, all right?" I lowered my voice again quickly, seeing heads rise in my periphery. After a steadying breath, I whispered my reply. "I certainly wouldn't have told anyone about it because I don't want you thinking I didn't care about Silas, but no . . . I wouldn't have rejected him. I'd have sent him an open invitation myself if I were free to."

I swallowed, feeling a strange ache in my chest now that I'd admitted it out loud.

Scarlet's hand was on mine. "I know, in my heart of hearts, that if Silas were here, you'd have devoted your life to his happiness. I know you to be loyal and caring, almost to a fault. You mustn't hold it against yourself that you never had the opportunity to prove it. We certainly don't. You are free, Hollis."

"I'm not. It would hurt Mother, I just know it." I toyed with the ring on my finger, the one that she gave me, the one passed down from Jedreck himself. I'd earned the right to wear it by marrying her son. I couldn't just abandon it. "Besides, if Etan succeeds, he will be king. He will have to marry for advantage. He'll need to establish his line as fast as he can, and I'm sure every lord who vows to support him will expect him to marry an Isolten girl with an impressive lineage to back his up."

"*You're* an Isolten girl now, Hollis. And *you* have an impressive lineage."

I sighed. "That's not . . . why are you so adamant about this?"

She shrugged, grinning from ear to ear. "I already told you. We need something to celebrate. Besides"—she looked back to the room, keeping her tone quiet—"everyone's made a comment or two about how close you've become over this trip. I don't know how it happened, but it's enough of a change that everyone sees it. Perhaps not the full depth of it, but still. And when they mention it, it's always with a smile."

I considered this, that there was a chance that no one would hate me for falling for Etan. But I couldn't give in to gravity just yet. Their support comforted me, but I was still convinced he had no interest. He called me his friend, he didn't want to get married anyway, and if he ever did, there would be expectations.

It'd be better to keep the scraps of my heart to myself; some poor boy might want them eventually.

"I need to watch the gate, Scarlet. For now, I just need him to live."

She shook her head. "That doesn't support your case at all," she noted.

I sighed. She was right, of course. "Case or no case, it doesn't change what is fact."

"Don't be ridiculous, Hollis. Love is a fact."

TWENTY-EIGHT

I WAS UNTHINKABLY TIRED. BUT as I kept watch, all I felt was nervousness and excitement, a fear and hope intermingled, stirring in my heart and stomach and hands. That won out, and I never faltered. When the darkest part of the night came, I squinted, looking for a torch. And when the inky blue sky turned to purple and the purple turned to pink, all I could think was: *he's coming any minute now.* He had to, right? He had to have made it.

And then, when the anticipation might have been ready to kill me, a grayish line appeared on the horizon.

I sat up taller, and Scarlet, noticing my change in posture, shifted beside me, squinting.

"What is . . . ," I started.

"That's an army, Hollis," she replied in hushed wonder.

We watched a moment longer, just to be sure, to see the

outline of his face. It only took a second. And once they were all but on top of the gate, a trumpeter sounded. He arrived with appropriate fanfare.

"He's here!" I cried, as if the horn wouldn't have drawn everyone to the window. "Oh, he's here, and there are so many people with him!"

I had expected to be able to count the numbers behind him, but I was completely shocked by the men—and the occasional woman—riding and marching under a silver flag as they came upon the castle.

"He's all right!" Aunt Jovana said, her words breaking over tears, tears of a mother carrying quiet worry over her last living child.

"So regal," Mother whispered, awed by the sight of it all, and Scarlet could only nod in agreement.

Everyone gaped at the sheer size of Etan's army, but all I could see was him.

His posture was tall, and his face was unapologetic and unafraid. He wore no crown yet, and I was sure that even if one had been available, he wouldn't put it on before everything was said and done. But he was wearing armor now and looked far more regal in this lone ride to the castle than Quinten ever had.

"It's time," Uncle Reid said. "Straighten yourselves up. We're going down to greet Etan, and we need to alert the others."

I'd been in the same dress for more than a day now. And maybe red was the wrong color for the occasion, but it was too late to fix it. I raked my fingers through my hair, pulling it over one shoulder.

"You look lovely," Scarlet insisted. "I can see the worry in your eyes."

I swallowed. "There are bigger things. Come."

We followed Uncle Reid down the hallway, and I watched as he passed each room, knocking three quick raps on the doors. Lord and Lady Dinnsmor sprang out of one, and Julien's family—the Kahtris—came from another. As we neared the stairs, Lord Odvar, who'd greeted me so sweetly when he learned I was Silas's widow, was coming down with scores of people behind him. It seemed several families had harbored together overnight, and within a minute, we had an army of our own.

We came around the corner just as Etan reached the guards. Oh, he did look handsome.

"Drop your weapons," Etan commanded.

One bold guard called back to him. "No, sir! This is treason!"

Etan shook his head. "My good man, I almost wish it was. Sadly, it is King Quinten who has committed high treason. He has killed Her Majesty's family and my own, executing crime after crime against his subjects both high and low. I have letters in his own hand and with his seal to back up my claim, and, as a blood heir to this crown, I have come to see justice done. You may lay your weapons down now and join us, or you will die in vain attempting to stop me."

He was so precise with his words, so certain.

I waited for one of the guards to charge, for a fight to break out. But, instead, one dropped his spear and quietly walked over to join Etan. After that, three more did. Then, slowly, they all abandoned their posts. The men behind Etan cheered and welcomed the guards into their ranks, and with that, it seemed the last of those who could defend King Quinten were gone.

I let out a shaky breath, both thankful and impressed.

Turning atop his horse, Etan called out to those behind him. "My faithful Isoltens. I will go in alone and bring King Quinten down to face his charges in front of you, his people, to whom his life ought to be owed. I hope that he will come peacefully, that we might handle these matters in the open, as you have a right to know the truth about all of them. If he refuses, then I urge you, for Isolte, you must fight!"

A deafening roar went up. It sounded like the entirety of the country was out there behind him. Etan climbed off his horse, and I watched his eyes light up when they met mine.

In the midst of his ascent, he wasted a beautiful moment on me. He stood there, gazing at me, his eyes asking for me to support him, too. And I did. With all my heart, I did.

"Son!" Uncle Reid called, breaking the spell.

"Father. They backed me," he said in shock, taking him by the shoulders. "They came. So many. It feels like too many. I can't believe they came."

Uncle Reid placed his forehead against Etan's. "I can. Are you ready?"

"I think so . . . I worry he won't step down peacefully. I

don't want any unnecessary violence today."

"Don't worry, my son. Neither will he. Not now."

Etan nodded. "I want you by my side. And I want Hollis there, too. I want him to know just who has led to his undoing."

"Of course," Uncle Reid said.

Etan turned to me.

"I am with you," I vowed. "Always."

He smiled and turned to the main stairway. He marched up decisively, knowing exactly where he was going. I'd been wrong about the last of the guards dropping away. As we wound up the spiral staircase, we came upon a few more, but at the sight of Etan, some dropped their weapons while others just ran. Clearly, the crowd had been spotted.

There was no one stopping us from walking right into the king's quarters. Etan pushed the door open in a swift and easy move, his sword—Jedreck's sword—at the ready.

In the room, King Quinten sat, bent over at his desk, as Princess Phillipa stood beside him, hands tucked in front of her, unmistakable worry painting her face. Meanwhile, Quinten looked up, seemingly unsurprised by our arrival.

"King Quinten, you are hereby under arrest for gross acts of treason against your people. I am here to escort you outside, where your citizens will hold you accountable for your crimes. Following their condemnation, I will take your crown, as is my birthright as a descendant of Jedreck the Great."

"That birthright belongs to Prince Hadrian and his

offspring," Phillipa said, her voice wavering.

Right. It wasn't only Quinten who had to go, but Hadrian and Phillipa as well. And, while Quinten was clearly evil, I couldn't say as much for Hadrian. In many ways, I pitied him. But what else were we to do about his presence?

It turned out Quinten had an answer to that problem.

He sighed heavily as he rubbed at his forehead, looking up at us from his chair. "Fortunately for your claim, sir . . . my son died this morning."

TWENTY-NINE

Uncle Reid, Etan, and I all paused. In the midst of our triumph, this was a hard blow. Hadrian's only sin was being Quinten's son. What's more, it looked like this was crippling to Quinten. Perhaps he was pained to lose the final link in his line for the throne, but the way he swallowed hard and didn't want to look into our eyes hinted that he was equally pained to have lost his son.

"But, *but*," Phillipa said pointedly to Quinten, "I could be carrying his child as we speak."

"You're not," Etan replied flatly. "We know about that little plot, too."

She smashed her lips together angrily, turning to Quinten. "You made me so many promises."

"If you were stupid enough to believe them, that's really your problem, isn't it?"

Her face went red, not in embarrassment but in rage. Her chest heaved as she stood there, wordlessly demanding this wrong to be righted. Unfortunately for her, that would never happen.

"You will stand," Etan ordered. "And you will take up your crown. The people in the back need to be able to recognize you."

Quinten raised an eyebrow. "You must have brought an impressive crowd of witnesses."

"Not witnesses," Etan corrected him. "An army. Of men and women, poor and wealthy, all ready to finally call you to pay for the crimes you've been committing for decades."

He made no attempt to deny this, bothered only that he'd been cornered. His head was heavy, his posture weary. He stood, walking to the coronet resting on its indigo pillow. He ran his bent fingers over the sharp tips of gold, seeming to remember an entire reign in seconds. I wished I could have said he looked to be mournful, regretful. But no.

He placed it on his head and turned to Etan. "So quick to judge. Wait and see what you do when someone comes to challenge you. Because that will certainly happen now. You've set a precedent today. And when you show the slightest sign of weakness, they will do what they can to topple you. I hope I'll still be alive to see your mighty principles fall."

"Well, seeing as I have no intention of murdering my own subjects, I don't think I'll quite be in the same predicament as you," he replied defiantly.

Quinten was unmoved. "As I said, we'll see."

"Come. Your people await," Uncle Reid said, escorting King Quinten out the door.

"What about her?" I asked, nodding at Phillipa.

She stayed incredibly still, as if she might blend into the stone and be ignored.

Etan shook his head. "Let her go home and attempt to explain this to her family and kingdom. That will be its own punishment."

She swallowed, but she didn't look as if she felt spared by her sentence. I turned from her, falling in step beside Etan, with Uncle Reid holding King Quinten several steps ahead.

Etan whispered as we walked. "I can't say this to them, but I can to you: I'm terrified."

"You needn't be. They adore you."

He nodded absently, like he was trying to convince himself. "Stay with me? Even though you hate crowns, don't run off. Not yet."

He reached a trembling hand over as we got to the bottom of the stairway. I quickly reached back to give him a reassuring squeeze. "Sorry. If you're wearing a crown, that's the end of our friendship. I'll be in the back throwing rotten food at you."

He chuckled a little, and, as we reached the main doors, he let my hand go. The crowd was already making a shocking amount of noise, but I refrained from covering my ears. Etan jumped up on one of the cylindrical stones that lined the entryway, raising a hand to quiet the army before him.

I found Mother and Scarlet nearby, and I immediately took Scarlet's hand, watching to see how the moment we'd been working toward finally played out.

"Good people, by our laws, I come to you today with proof of our king's treasonous acts against our fellow Isoltens." Etan held a fistful of letters high. "In these, we have undeniable evidence that our king has ordered the murder of scores of his citizens. We have proof of the devious methods he's employed to hold on to his throne. His actions preclude him from ever wearing the crown again. Queen Valentina has renounced her crown and fled the country," he called, and Quinten looked up to him in shock. "And it has been brought to my attention that Prince Hadrian died this morning."

There was a murmuring through the crowd.

"As a descendant of Jedreck the Great, I stand before you today to claim my right to the throne of Isolte, and to ask your blessing as I take it from this unjust man." Etan pointed to Quinten. I supposed he was a king no more.

The crowd cheered, ready to be done with the years of absolute terror. When they had all but quieted down, one brave soul shouted out above the crowd, "Justice for the Eastoffes!" and the cry went up again.

At this, Quinten, whose head had been low under the blows of losing his wife, his son, and his throne in one fell swoop, stood up straight, raising a hand. "I will admit that I have done plenty of things over the years some might call criminal. I'm sure that, very soon, I will be forced to tell a committee all about them. But the Eastoffes' blood is not on my hands."

I felt the tension in Scarlet's body change completely through the touch of her hand, and Mother staggered a breath before calling out, "Liar!"

"No, no," Quinten insisted. "Did I have Valentina's family killed? Yes. It had to happen. Lord Erstwhell, Lord Swithins . . . a whole family on the coast . . . I've had so many people killed in the name of my own peace, I can't count them. But Sir Eastoffe? That upstart Silas?" He shook his head. "I can't take credit for that."

We stood silently. I clutched the rings at my throat. He admitted to his crimes so easily. Why would he deny this one . . . unless he was telling the truth?

"If you didn't, then who did?" Scarlet demanded.

"Took me a while to figure it out myself," Quinten said. For the multitudes standing before us, we might have been able to hear a pin fall to the ground for how quietly and intently we were all listening to find the truth behind their deaths. "But it all makes sense now. If you want to know, you should ask her."

And I froze in horror as Quinten tipped his chin at me.

THIRTY

"How dare you?" I shouted, nearly dizzy with anger. "I loved Silas! I have *nothing* to do with his death!"

"Oh, but you do, dear girl. You have everything to do with it." Quinten spoke so calmly. "Don't mistake me. I was relieved to find out the Eastoffe line was all but dead, but I didn't know it had happened until you walked into my palace and told me about it."

"I still don't understand," I rasped, hysterical tears threatening to take over in the midst of such a wild accusation. "I didn't kill Silas."

He smiled at me cruelly. "Can you not think of anyone in this world who would want that boy dead more than I would?"

The edges of my vision went blurry as my body started

shaking. Yes. Yes, I could think of someone who would want Silas Eastoffe dead.

"Jameson," I whispered.

After I uttered the word aloud, the people in the crowd picked it up, whispering to one another, carrying it until everyone knew.

Of course it was Jameson. It explained so much. Why no one in Isolte had heard about the Eastoffes' dying in the first place. Why he knew to send my widow's fund so quickly.

"Oh," Scarlet mumbled, covering her mouth and shaking her head. "Oh, Hollis. He had a ring." She looked at me, another piece of her picture coming into perfect clarity. "The man who grabbed me back at Abicrest. He had one of those rings, like your father had. The Coroan rings. I didn't remember it until now. And, *and*! He let me go." She gripped at her hair, looking ready to pull it out.

"So?"

"He thought I was you!" she said, finally bringing sense to the moment. "You were supposed to be the only one who made it out alive."

So, this was Jameson's plan. He found out about Silas and eliminated him—eliminated everyone—hoping my desperation would drive me back to the palace. Instead it drove me to Isolte.

"So, now you know," Quinten said, looking so pleased with himself. He smirked, looking smug even in his downfall. "And, interestingly enough, if the Eastoffes were *truly*

Coroan citizens, it would seem Jameson is just as guilty as I am. Do you intend to take his crown as well? Throw him in a dungeon?"

My blood was turning to ice, making my body go numb as it traveled. Jameson. All this time, it was him.

"Silence!" Etan ordered. "If King Jameson has crimes to atone for, we will address that in the future." He looked to me, clearly pained to see what this did to me, to be so deceived by someone who claimed to love me. "Today we are here to discuss your crimes and your crown. You just freely admitted to killing Her Majesty's family and several other courtiers by name. You will kneel and relinquish your crown. Now!"

Some restless soul called out, "Off with his head!" and a second later, most of the crowd had joined in.

Quinten looked sideways at Etan, reaching up to remove the coronet. He handed it over to Uncle Reid wordlessly, standing there and awaiting his fate.

The people were thirsty for blood, and I couldn't blame them. Quinten had listed their friends and neighbors by name, admitted there was much more. But I wondered what would become of so much violence.

The fear in Etan's eyes had returned. What was he to do now? The crown was hanging between his head and Quinten's, and his new people were making demands. I watched as he drew Jedreck's sword from its sheath, holding it in his hand with perfect control. I waited for him to come down from his perch, to kill Quinten in one clean stroke. I had no doubt he could do it.

Instead, he turned and faced the massive army, holding the sword in the air, demanding silence.

"By law, this man must have a trial. None of us here are fit to stand jury, so we will assemble one from nobles in neighboring countries to offer the fairest treatment we can. Furthermore, he has given the command in many of these murders, but they were done at the hands of the group you and I know as the Darkest Knights. We need names, and only he can provide them. We will not act in anger now; not when we know we can do better. When people speak of this moment, they will speak of how we acted justly, and nothing more." He turned to a handful of guards. "Escort him to the dungeon; we'll deal with him in due course."

He spoke with such authority that if he told me the law required anything, I'd have believed him. And he looked so regal, so princely atop that stone, sword in his hand, that no one dared to question him.

"Son?" Uncle Reid said quietly. Etan turned to him. "It's time."

Etan nodded, swallowing hard before jumping off the stone. He looked at me, his eyes still nervous. I gave him a quick smile and nodded, trying to tell him to just get on with it. He knelt to the ground, the sword still in his hand, driving the tip into the ground like a crutch.

Etan looked up to his father and then bowed his head.

"Etan Northcott, son of Reid Northcott, descendant of Jedreck the Great, do you give your word that you will serve and protect the people of Isolte as its king?"

"All of them. Even unto death," Etan vowed.

Uncle Reid placed the crown upon Etan's head. "Arise, King Etan."

He stood, looking somehow even taller, and the crowd exploded into jubilant cheers. Taking deep breaths, Etan climbed back up on the rock to see out into the crowd, and the cheers grew even louder as everyone in the back could now see he wore the crown.

"My p—" Etan started, but he had to stagger out a breath. He put his hand to his heart and looked near tears when he spoke again. "My people. I thank you for your support. I cannot express my joy in the knowledge that good was done today, and not a single drop of your blood was spilled to attain it. We have much to celebrate!

"I invite as many of you who would like to please stay. We will open the palace stores and commemorate the day. To any who are unable to stay, I pray that as you travel home, you share the news of what has happened here, and pass on my blessings to every subject in Isolte."

There was more cheering as people moved into the palace and spread across the lawn. Etan was enveloped by people, and I watched as he smiled in disbelief as person after person congratulated him.

King Etan. It suited him.

In the rush, it was all too easy to take his horse and march quietly through the sea of people, moving against the flow. It wasn't until I was well outside the palace walls that the crowds somewhat dispersed and I could climb atop Etan's horse.

When I'd thought Quinten had killed my husband, I'd only wanted one thing: to look into his eyes as he confessed his sins. And now, I would have that from Jameson.

I dug my heels into the horse, and we bolted.

THIRTY-ONE

I HOPED I WAS HEADING in the right direction. There was one large road out of the city, and once it branched off, I assumed the one heading west would veer north and take me up to Coroa. I was too blinded by my heartache to think of anything but getting to Keresken Castle.

When I'd left, Jameson had said that I'd come back to him. Did he know even then about Silas? Did he at least suspect? I felt certain that Silas was a well-kept secret until after we were gone. Was he simply prepared to set fire to any other path my life might lead me down so long as the one back to him was clear?

I thought of all the others who'd died in this farce. Jameson knew about the Darkest Knights and wanted to mimic them to hide his own monstrous deeds. Because he wanted Silas to die, so did everyone at our wedding. Mother was spared because we were in the garden, and Scarlet was only alive because my hair was a little too close to Isolten blonde.

Tears blurred my vision as I pressed on. I didn't know what lay before me. I didn't have a plan. If I accused Jameson, what exactly did I expect to happen? He wouldn't admit to it, but I had no doubts now that all of the pieces were in place. But, even if he confessed to me, nothing was going to happen to him. Unlike Quinten, he hadn't wronged most of his countrymen. Jameson was young, charming, beloved. Furthermore, he had no one to challenge him for his throne, so even if he was to lose it, it would make things worse for Coroa. . . .

What was I doing? I was powerless. I had no army, no proof. I had the word of a deposed king and a stolen horse.

But, in the depths of myself, I knew I'd never know peace again until I went to Jameson, looked in his eyes, and demanded the truth. For better or worse, I had to keep going.

I rode on, noting how quickly the sun was moving and thinking of the carriage ride to the palace a week ago. I'd had a similar feeling in my gut, like I was moving closer and closer to the thing that might kill me. The difference then was that Mother and Scarlet were riding ahead of me. And Etan was beside me.

Oh, Etan. How I wanted to kick him in his shins every time I saw him. The thought brought a smile to my lips. I just wanted to one-up him at everything. Little chance of that now. Hard to get better than being king.

He was going to do so well. He had good parents to guide him, a purpose to direct his passion toward. He had the skill to curb anger and enough wit to disarm anyone daring enough to get close to him.

He was going to absolutely flourish.

I thought of that string in my chest, the one that pulled me to Silas, the one that pulled me to Mother and Scarlet. That thread was now fully unspooled at the feet of Etan Northcott, and I imagined nothing would tug at my heart ever again.

In a way, I wanted to mourn—certainly this was the end of so many things for me. But I was also so grateful. I'd finally gone somewhere. I'd built a family. Even if I failed in Coroa, I'd helped bring justice for those in Isolte. I'd loved, and I'd been loved. It was all more than I'd imagined myself capable of. So I rode into the unknown with doubt in my heart, but my head held high.

What was that?

I heard something that sounded like a rumbling storm. The sky around me still looked clear, and even when I surveyed the fields in front of me, nothing was there. Where was that noise coming from? What *was* that sound?

"Hollis!"

I pulled the horse to a dead stop, turning in disbelief.

On the horizon, Etan was coming, full speed, coronet on his head, and his army behind him.

My eyes welled.

He'd come for me.

"Hollis!"

I waved back to him, telling him I was waiting. He raised his hand, and the mass of men on horses behind him came to a stop as he carried on, coming to meet me.

He stopped as we faced one another atop our horses, staring at each other.

"Hello," he finally said.

And I laughed. "Etan Northcott, you idiot—"

"King Idiot to you, thank you."

"—what are you doing here?"

He sighed, looking at me as if it were obvious. "My dearest friend, who usually, mind you, is very bright, decided to ride off—alone—and confront a king for something he undoubtedly did, but for which she has no proof. Alone. And my guess is she actually has no idea how to proceed once she gets there. And did I mention she was alone?"

"You did."

"Ah, well. Then you see why I had to come."

I shook my head. "You can't go with me to Coroa. You've been king for, what, a few hours? Go home."

"And you cannot run off to face Jameson on your own," he replied. "I knew you were a bit ridiculous, but this is too much, even for you."

I rolled my eyes. "This is how we're doing this? You're just going to insult me?"

"It seems if I do it enough, you see reason. So, yes. Also, your hair looks terrible."

"What?" I asked, reaching up to touch it.

He smirked. "I'm joking. You look like a goddess riding into battle. You're glorious."

I put my hand down, shaking my head and smiling against my wishes. I looked over his shoulder to the army behind him.

"I can't ask you to come with me. I can't ask *them* to come with me. This isn't their fight."

"You're not asking," he said. "*I* didn't even ask them. I announced where I was going, and . . ." He gestured to the throngs of men behind him.

"Really?"

He nodded. "Besides, as the widow of an Isolten citizen, and in a sense an extended member of the royal family—"

"Barely. Not even by blood."

"No, not by blood. By an hour of marriage. Yes, I understand the terms of your arrival. Still, you are under my rule. And you are under my protection. You're an Isolten, Hollis. And I won't let you face your enemy alone. I won't let you do anything alone."

I batted back the tears. My heart was allowing me to make too much of those words, and I wanted to hate it for that. Instead, I did what I always did with Etan. I argued.

"I remember someone saying I would never be Isolten."

He shrugged. "It was easier than admitting you already were."

We stayed there a moment, horses shifting beneath us, watching each other's eyes.

"I'm going whether you like it or not. In the same way you have been both Coroan and Isolten, so was my uncle, so were my cousins. Killing one's own subjects is evil, and Jameson ought to be held responsible."

I swallowed. "We may not walk out alive."

"If that's the case, then I'll fall beside you. And Scarlet will be queen. And I will be happier in my death than I ever thought I could be."

I let out a shaky breath.

"Good luck keeping up. This horse is fast." I pulled the reins and started moving.

"That's because he's mine!" he protested, lifting his hand to move the army.

We rode wordlessly, Etan right beside me and his army not far behind. I didn't mind that we said nothing; there was a great comfort in being silent with Etan. It allowed my mind room to wander, to test out courses of action. I kept thinking of how I needed to address Jameson. If he was as desperate to see me as Quinten claimed, then he'd surely take me somewhere alone, away from the eyes of court to greet me properly. I could ask him about the attack then, maybe even lie and say I was flattered he'd do something so grand for my sake. If I could just get him to confess to me, that was enough to bring a case against him. As a fellow monarch, Etan could do that.

I just had to get that far.

But the first hitch in my plan showed up at the border:

a Coroan patrol, with wide barricades that stretched down into the tree lines, making it impossible to pass through unseen.

"I have an idea," I said to Etan. He merely nodded as we pulled up to a halt.

One of the men crossed in front of the barricade, his flat palm telling me to stop, though I already had.

"What's the meaning of this?" he demanded, motioning to the wave of people behind us.

"Sir, my name is Hollis East—"

"Lady Hollis?" he asked. "How . . . why were you in Isolte?"

"I had an urgent matter to attend to, and I return on one equally important. King Quinten has been relieved of his crown. His relative, King Etan, has taken his place only this morning. Knowing the relationship with Coroa to be of the utmost importance, he's come to meet with King Jameson immediately. We request passage right away."

The guard looked between me and Etan, pausing to take in the circle of gold upon his head.

"He will want to see him," I insisted.

The guard grumbled to himself a bit. "He can pass, but not that lot." He pointed to the army behind us.

"For His Majesty's safety, he must be allowed some men. You know as well as I that Isoltens are not always taken to kindly. And it's still quite the journey to Keresken Castle."

He sighed. "Ten."

"One hundred," I countered.

He shook his head. "I ~~don't need~~ to barter with you, my lady."

I pulled my head high, using what bravado I could muster. "But you do. Surely you know my place in King Jameson's life. If I am traveling with someone from Isolte, I must be secure as well." I kept my nose in the air, my tone calm and sure.

The guard huffed. "Twenty."

"Fifty."

He frowned. "Fifty, then. Go on."

Etan trotted back to the men, speaking quietly as a group of fifty was divided from the rest of the crowd. When they were decided upon, we made our way over the Coroan border. But as we passed into my homeland, I looked back at all those men who had not only stood for Etan this morning but were willing to stand for me now. I blew them a kiss, and they silently raised their swords in the air in salute.

It looked like they had no intention of leaving until we came back with word.

"Are you sure you don't have a king somewhere in your family tree, too?" Etan asked.

"What? No. Why do you ask?"

"Because if I hadn't known any better, I'd have taken a knee to you back there."

He smiled and moved to lead his men as we went to right the last wrong.

THIRTY-TWO

WE RODE OVER THE COUNTRYSIDE at top speed, only slowing when we could see the towering shape of Keresken Castle in the distance. I looked upon it with new eyes. The river where I'd lost my shoes felt like a threatening moat, the city folk more like nosy acquaintances than welcoming allies. And that castle . . .

The place where I'd done so much living and breathing, the place where Delia Grace became my best friend and I fell in love with Silas, the place where I'd danced and slept and hoped . . . from here it looked like a cell.

"Are you all right?" Etan asked, breaking me from my thoughts.

I swallowed and nodded. "I'm scared to go back in there."

"Hey," he said, forcing me to look his way. "You are not walking in alone. And if we can confront one king and have it end in peace, then there's no reason why we can't confront two."

I wished I could believe that was true. But I now saw Jameson the way I had always seen Quinten: If he was capable of something so cold and cruel, how could I trust him to show any mercy to me?

We crossed the bridge and made our way to the winding road that led up to the castle. At the sight of such a gathering of men, some women who ran shops along the main street clutched the hands of their children and pulled them inside, while others looked at my face, doing double takes, unsure if they were truly seeing the woman who'd jilted their king.

I glanced over at Etan, who seemed completely at ease, riding up to Keresken with one hand on the reins and the other on his hip, not bothering to look back at his men, but simply trusting they were behind him. So sure, so calm. I took a cue from him and pulled my posture up as we laced through the last of the town and moved toward the entryway of the castle. The space that had been filled with carriages the night Silas and I ran was empty now, and two guards stood at the door while another two kept watch at the edges of the plain.

They were surprised, of course, and raised their spears at our approach. "Halt!" they commanded.

"I assure you, your king wants to meet the new king of Isolte," Etan said, standing tall on his horse, the coronet shining in the setting sun. "Stand aside. I have an urgent message for His Majesty. And my men outnumber you, should you be foolish enough to disobey my command."

Chills went up my arms at his words. I watched as the guards looked at one another, unsure. After some hurried whispers, one looked forward. "The men have to stay here."

Etan nodded, and they let us pass. Just inside the gates, Etan and I both dismounted, tying the horses to a post. He scratched both of their noses before turning and standing tall. He held out his arm . . . and I just stared at it.

"What? A lady needs an escort. Might as well walk in on the arm of a king," he said, his cocky tone back in full force.

I sighed, putting my hand on his and asked a question that I hated to ask but that my vanity demanded of me. "Don't lie. How do I look?"

Etan's face instantly softened. "Absolutely radiant. Like the moon," he said quietly. "Sure and determined, reflecting light on everyone around you, and so desperately beautiful to those who don't even realize they're in the dark."

I ran my hands over my knotted, windswept hair. "Really?"

"Absolutely."

I closed my eyes and turned beside Etan to make our way into the castle. I took a few deep breaths as we walked, trying to focus my thoughts. I knew what I needed to say, but I feared none of it would come out right. I was going to give them—my parents, Silas, all those innocent bystanders—my best or die trying.

"By the way," Etan began as we entered the hall, our footsteps echoing in the grand entryway, "I realize I said

I'd never go near an altar, and I maintain that you are an obnoxious brat . . . but I will love you to the very last beat of my heart."

He looked into my eyes, gaze unwavering. My breath caught for a second, but my reply had been waiting to be said for so long that it came out easily.

"I know I said I'd never go near a crown, and I believe you are far too full of yourself . . . but I will love you to the very end."

We turned into the Great Hall, catching everyone mid-dinner. There were people dancing in the middle of the floor, girls looping arms around one another and spinning as Delia Grace and I had so many times in our childhood. Speaking of my dear old friend, there she was at the head table, just to Jameson's left. She was bedecked in enough jewels to crush a man and laughing as I'd never heard her laugh before at something or other Jameson had said.

Etan and I walked calmly into the room, pausing at the back. It only took seconds for people to take in my face and his crown. The commotion began at the back of the hall and worked its way forward. The dancers stepped aside, and shocked fingers pointed our way. Eventually it got so distracting that the music stopped from the gallery above, and Jameson finally noted us.

He stared at us for a moment, trying to put together how two people could upend an entire room. Then his eyes met mine, searching me over to be sure.

"Hollis? Hollis Brite, is that you?"

Beside him, I watched all the joy in Delia Grace's eyes melt away, and I hated knowing I was the cause of it.

"I knew you'd come back to me," he said in a low voice. "In the end, I knew you would."

Of course you did, I thought. *You orchestrated it that way.*

Etan's hand was still under mine, and he ran his thumb reassuringly over my fingers. I took a breath and let go of him.

"Your Majesty, I would like to introduce you to His Majesty, King Etan Northcott of Isolte," I greeted him, gesturing to Etan.

Jameson's eyes went wide in delight. "Are you telling me the old man finally died? And Hadrian as well?"

"Prince Hadrian died this morning," I informed him. "The former king was deposed by his highest-ranking relative and is currently imprisoned for treason."

Jameson leaned his head back and laughed. He *laughed.*

"Even better. Oh, Your Majesty, you are quite welcome here. Please, join in our feast! I shall have plates and chairs brought, and we can celebrate the new king of Isolte and the return of my dear Hollis."

Jameson nodded to the pages to snap to work. I held up a hand, and, to my surprise, Jameson stilled. He stared at me in shock.

"Before anything else, I must speak to you," I demanded. "There are certain actions that I must have answers for. There will be no celebration between us because there is no peace between us. And I will not dine with you without it."

He chuckled, tilting his head to the side. "Hollis Brite," he said sweetly, "I have clothed you and fed you. I have commanded my countrymen and foreigners alike to treat you as a queen. I let your all-but-common head wear royal jewels." His voice was growing louder as he spoke. "And when you rejected this kindness, when you asked to leave, I let you go without a fight. On what grounds can you possibly claim I have given you anything but peace?!"

"Shall I say it?" I demanded, stepping away from Etan, though I could feel him walking up behind me. "Should I tell your court what you really are?"

"And what am I?"

"A murderer!" I shouted in a voice so strong it felt like the stones in the wall shook.

The silence between us was so very charged, so painfully loud. I could feel the eyes of every single person flickering between Jameson and me, desperately curious about how this would end.

"I beg your pardon?" he asked so coolly.

In a steady voice, I said it again. "You are a murderer, Jameson Barclay. Crown or no, you are as wretched as a common criminal. And you ought to be on your knees from the weight of your shame."

Someone near me swallowed.

After a moment, the ice in Jameson's eyes softened, and he smiled at me. "My Lady Hollis, based on your appearance, I would guess you've been through quite a traumatic day. I don't know what you think—"

"I don't *think* anything. I *know* you had Silas Eastoffe murdered. I *know* you had my parents murdered. I know it was your men at my wedding, and the blood of your people is on your hands."

Etan's slow breaths were right beside me.

Jameson tilted his head again. "Because of the great love I've had for you, I am willing to let these false allegations against me die. But I warn you, any more lies, and I will not be so generous."

"They. Are not. Lies," I insisted calmly.

"Where's your proof?" he asked, spreading his arms wide. "I am willing to bet I have far more incriminating evidence about you than you do about me."

He signaled to one of the holy men, standing near the door to his chambers. "Bring me that parchment on my desk with the gold seal." Jameson looked back to me before darting his eyes over to Etan. "And my sword, too," he called after.

"You were the only one in all of Coroa or Isolte who acknowledged their deaths and my widowhood," I continued, ignoring his little show. "Because you were the only one who knew. The sole person who made it out of the room was my sister-in-law, Scarlet. And that was only because my hair looks closer to Isolten blonde than Coroan brunette. The men who took down our guests were wearing silver rings, the rings of Coroan nobility. The men who killed my family are probably standing in this room." My voice started to shake, my anger and sorrow mixing into something bigger than I could hold.

"Breathe," Etan whispered.

I did.

"This is all circumstantial, Hollis. It proves nothing." He said it all with such composure, as if he'd known this day might come, and he'd had this speech prepared. "If anyone here has cause for wielding accusations, it's me. And if anyone here has broken a law, it's you. Because, unlike you, I have things in writing. I have proof that you, my lady, never should have gotten married at all. Seeing as you were already married to me."

THIRTY-THREE

THERE WERE GASPS AROUND THE room, but I stood there unmoved, as I knew this to be a magnificent lie. A second later, the holy man reappeared. In his hands, he held two things. The first, a rolled-up scroll with a golden seal. The second, a sword. But it wasn't any old sword Jameson had in his vast collection. It had a golden blade and jewels encrusted in the hilt.

He meant to threaten me with something made by Silas's hand.

"Do you know what this is?" Jameson asked with a smirk, holding up the scroll.

I had no answer.

After a short silence, he broke the golden seal and opened it, showing a very long document with several signatures on it.

"Hollis, I wanted you for my bride from very early in our courtship. I knew you would be mine. But you were so green, so rough, that I understood it would take time to make people come around and see you as I did." He laughed. "Look at you now! Even in such a state, you look ready for a throne, regal and shining like the sun."

"I am not the sun," I muttered, but he ignored me.

"I had to have you. But seeing as the law made us wait, I bent the law to me. Your parents were kind enough to oblige."

My heart stopped beating. No. No, they couldn't have.

"I'm sure from there you might not be able to see the date on this," Jameson said, "but if we look right . . . here." He pointed to a line. "Why, what's that? Oh, it's the date of Crowning Day."

"What is that thing, Hollis?" Etan asked quietly.

"A contract. My parents signed me into a betrothal. They're formal, complicated, and the only one who can void them is the king," I said, looking over to Etan, feeling absolutely defeated. "According to that paper, I'm married to him. I've been married to him since the night I ran away."

"There you have it, Hollis," Jameson said finally. "You are mine. And now you will be made to yield to the law. And you will take your place beside me . . . as I always said you would." He turned to Delia Grace, who'd been sitting there quietly this whole time. When she stayed there gripping the arms of her chair in shock, he said, "You can go."

After watching her be repeatedly degraded through the

years, I felt the deepest shame that her most public humiliation unwittingly came at my hands. For better or worse, Delia Grace had been my sole companion for most of my life, and she had a measure of my love no one could steal.

Her tears fell silently as she rose from her seat, curtsied to Jameson, and walked to the side of the room. In an unexpected act of kindness, Nora was waiting off to the side with open arms, embracing her as she came down. Delia Grace stood there, facing the wall as Nora held her, trying to hide her face from the crowd.

"Anytime, Hollis," he said, gesturing to the space beside him.

Here I was, being commanded by the king to take my place beside him, a place my parents, in their best hopes, secured for their only daughter. Oh, their rage when I refused to go back the palace with them made so much sense now. What else could they have done?

"Move, woman."

I heard Etan growl beside me.

"I am giving you a command, Hollis Brite!"

And it was that, his third refusal to address me by my married name, that made me snap. I stared down that wicked man and held my head high. "You'll find my name is Hollis Eastoffe now, and that I am a citizen of Isolte. You do not command me. I never have and never will belong to you!"

Jameson was standing there behind his massive head table, all alone.

"Hollis, I want to be a good husband to you. Generous,

kind. But you are not setting us up for a very happy marriage."

"I don't want to be married to you!" I shouted.

"But you already are!" he screamed back, the veins in his neck and temple bulging grotesquely as he slammed the scroll onto the table. "So I suggest you behave."

"And what if she simply refuses?" Etan asked calmly. "As a king in my own right, I can offer this lady a level of protection in my court it seems she will be lacking in yours."

"Who are you to speak to me?" Jameson asked.

Etan, undeterred, replied. "I just told you. A fellow sovereign. And if the way you casually dismissed that young lady," he said, tipping his forehead at Delia Grace, "is any indication of how women are treated in your court, I will take Lady Hollis Eastoffe home with me now."

Jameson raised his sword—Silas's sword—and pointed it at Etan. "Is this usurper what you would leave me for?" he bellowed.

"I would leave you for a pauper," I replied spitefully. "You are a murderous coward, and I will not be your wife."

He stood on his chair. "It is done!" he insisted. "You cannot fight it. You cannot fight me!" He climbed up over the table, preparing to come at Etan and me in his rage.

Etan drew his sword, but it made no difference.

For as fast as it all happened, the moment itself felt drawn out, as if I could see each piece fall into place almost before it occurred.

Jameson, in his anger and urgency, lost his footing as he

jumped from the table. He tripped, dropping his golden sword. The setting sun glinted across the blade as it fell, and all I could think was that Silas's work looked lovely, even when it was tumbling. The sword landed on its hilt, tipped up toward Jameson. And when he stumbled off the edge of his dais, his proud platform where he could survey those who worshipped him, the blade pierced him through.

I saw the way it lined up with his body, knew that there was no way to save him from his own mistake, and I turned my face into Etan's chest. For all the pain Jameson had wrought, I didn't want to see any more death. I stayed there for a moment, wishing I could also block the shouts from around the room and the anguished sounds of Jameson gurgling as he died. When everything finally went quiet, I turned.

Jameson lay there in a pool of his own blood, a golden sword through his chest.

A holy man went over to him and placed a hand beneath his nose, feeling for a breath. When nothing happened, he rose.

"The king is dead," he called out. "Long live the queen."

And I stood in silence as an entire room of nobles looked to me.

THIRTY-FOUR

BESIDE ME, ETAN WENT TO a knee. Kissing my hand and then touching it to his temple, he whispered, "Your Majesty."

A tremble rose from my toes and went all the way to the ends of my hair.

In an instant the holy men were beside me as the guards carefully escorted the courtiers from the Great Hall. Many were shielding their faces from the sight of a dead body, and many more were speaking furtively, trying to understand how so much had happened in such a few moments.

"Your Majesty, you must come with us. There is much to discuss," a holy man said.

They meant me. *I* was Your Majesty. I drew in a ragged breath. I was, in the most bureaucratic sense, Jameson's wife. And, as his wife on paper, I was queen. And, as he had no heirs, that meant the crown went to me. But of all the ways

I'd imagined this day ending, none had led me to this, and I couldn't wrap my mind around being in possession of a kingdom.

Numbly, I nodded. I turned to Etan, expecting him to follow.

He smiled kindly. "I'm sorry, Hollis. I don't think these gentlemen want a foreign king here as they discuss matters of state with their very new queen. Besides . . . I have a kingdom of my own awaiting my return."

"But . . ." No. There was no but. He was right.

Etan pulled my hand to his lips again. "When things have settled, we will talk. But know that you will always have an ally in Isolte."

How was I supposed to let him go? After everything we'd been through, after everything we'd finally said, how was I supposed to go even a minute without him?

"Etan . . . I can't . . ."

"Yes, you can. Look at everything you've already done," he assured me. "Go. Do what you must. Even if I'm gone, you are not alone in this. You have my support, Isolte's support. I will tell everyone at home of your new reign, and I will write you as soon as I can."

My hand was still in his. He was waiting.

I had to be the one to let go.

I squeezed it tight one last time and put my hands by my side. It took everything I had not to cry in front of him. I sank into a curtsy, and he bowed in return.

And then he dashed from the room, from the castle, from my world.

"Your Majesty," the same holy man said urgently. "Please come with me. There is much I need to tell you. Alone."

"I hope one day you might forgive me for my part in this," the holy man—Langston—said. "We all owe you the deepest of apologies."

I picked up the paper again, looking it over in disbelief. In Jameson's handwriting, the letter detailed when and where my wedding was to take place and spelled out the mission of the men he'd hired. I'd been wrong about the men killing my family possibly being in the Great Hall. He'd specifically gone for nobility who still had names but no fortunes, people who would be his allies based on status but in desperate need of money based on their circumstances. The sums he paid each of them—also detailed in the letter—would be enough to redeem an entire family.

"I never ought to have served these papers. But I felt duty bound to obey my king. I *suspected* what was in them, but I wasn't sure. I saved this one, just in case. Once I heard what happened to your husband, I broke the seal and read it myself. Then I knew one day this letter would be imperative to making a case against the king. I hid it away, praying it was never found unless someone who could make the whole matter right came forward. So now, please let me be a part in finding justice, even if that costs me my own life."

It took me a moment to realize he was waiting for me to speak. I cleared my throat, trying to think.

"Based on my sister Scarlet's account, some of these men died and were burned in the fire. That is enough punishment on their families. We will need to collect the others for questioning. Except the last one, the one you kept this letter from."

He nodded.

"As for you, I know firsthand how compelling Jameson could be. And you were, as you said, trying to do your duty. I want the men capable of murdering their countrymen brought to justice, but otherwise, I'd like to set the whole matter to rest."

He bowed his head. "That is very generous, Your Majesty."

I shook my head. "Must you call me that? I wasn't born royal; this doesn't feel right at all."

He pulled out the law books and the tidy little contract my parents had signed one more time. "His Majesty was the last of his line. He has no relatives to speak of, no one who has a legitimate claim to the throne. Except for you.

"Perhaps not in practice or deed, but on paper, you were his wife. I cannot force you to take the crown—no one can—but I must beg you to consider the outcome if you do not. We could risk civil war as usurpers try to take the throne. And if there isn't a clear, singular leader, neighboring countries might invade, attempt to take the land and claim it as their own. We could lose *Coroa*."

I stood, walking to the window as I considered this. My mother used to say to wait for daylight when there was a decision to be made. There was none of that to help me now. The moon was peeking up from behind the horizon. She would have to do.

How had Etan described the moon? Reflecting light back? A guide for those who didn't know they were in the dark?

Whatever he'd said, it was beautiful.

Could I really be like that? Could I be a guide? Could I be a light?

Could I lead Coroa?

I'd loved so many things in my life. I'd loved my freedom. I'd loved my family. I'd loved dancing and showing off my gowns. I'd loved gaining a sister. I'd loved Silas. I'd loved Etan.

Some of those loves were much shallower than others, but the thought of making every love I could ever have for all my life come in second place to Coroa . . . it was frightening.

If I said yes, it meant closing the door on so many things, on a thousand possibilities for my future. It meant service and humility and a lifetime of correcting wrongs.

And if I said no, it meant risking Coroa.

I had been scared to come back here, but I realized now that so much of that fear was tied to Jameson. And he was gone. Without him, all I could think of was that someone had to protect this land, the land that Queen Honovi made the boundaries of with her kisses, the one Queen Albrade protected on horseback.

I couldn't leave Coroa by the wayside, risking her falling into the hands of someone who might break her or suppress her. No. I would never let that happen.

When I turned around, the holy man was standing there, the Crown of Estus in his hands.

And I took a knee.

THREE
MONTHS
LATER

THIRTY-FIVE

I walked around the table a second time. "No, no." I pointed to the flowers in the middle. "In Isolte, these are used in mourning. Replace them. I think that's everything."

"Yes, Your Majesty," the page said eagerly. "And the menu?"

"It's all been approved. If you have any further questions, they may be directed to my principal lady."

The butlers and pages bowed and moved, finishing up all the final details. There was only one thing left to take care of, and it *should* be done by the end of the day. If everyone was on task, that is.

I walked from the chamber we'd been using for planning and into the central corridor of the castle. Unlike the kings before me, I preferred to work where I might see my people. There were bows and curtsies as I made my way out toward the courtyard. As expected, all the young girls were working on one big dance together, with Nora choreographing. I'd never seen anything quite so large, and I was sure it would impress.

Nora caught me watching and asked with her eyes what I thought. I gave her a warm smile and a satisfied nod. It really looked beautiful.

It had been her idea to have the young girls do something together, and I appreciated it. How much happier would my early years at court have been if we'd tried to build something as a group instead of feeling like we had to compete all the time?

As I watched, lulled into a stupor by the twirling gowns, a page approached. "Morning post, Majesty."

"Thank you . . . It was Andrews, was it not?"

He smiled. "Yes, Your Majesty." He moved on quickly, and I scanned the names on the letters to see what had come. The first several were from lords, and I'd need to see my council before responding to any of them. At the very back were three meant not for the queen, but for Hollis . . . well, maybe one of them was meant for the queen. I tucked inside the low wall of the palace and bent over, reading away.

> *Your Majesty,*
> *You will be pleased to know that the last teaching position was filled this morning. We now have suitable instructors for all subjects. As of last week, all the rooms in Varinger Hall have students assigned to them, so in the next week or so,*

we will begin the courses you laid out. The staff has been preparing around the clock, and while it's not the work any of us signed up for, everyone is delighted to be useful again and to see the manor full of life.

The first girl arrived this week. We have three orphans coming, and she is one. She was so timid, but the maids have taken her in like a little kitten, and I feel certain once she's able to meet her classmates, she will blossom.

The manor is in good hands. I am seeing to all the grounds and house, and the headmistress you chose is an agreeable woman who is very organized. I feel certain that if you get to visit, which we all very much hope you do, that you will be pleased with this school. We will keep you informed of any issues we have as things begin, but I'm very hopeful for the future of this project.

It is a brilliant idea, Your Majesty. One day, Coroa will be filled with schools like these, and the future citizens will have you to thank for it.

We pray for your health and reign. Visit soon.

Your humble servant,

Hester

Finally, that giant old house was serving some kind of purpose. I wasn't sure if a live-in school for country children would work, but we wouldn't know if we didn't try. I had no illusions of myself being someone who walked into war or saved countless sick . . . but I could do little bits of good a little bit at a time, and I hoped that when the end of my reign came, that would be what people remembered.

I moved on to the second letter.

Your Majesty,

Hollis,

I am finding Great Perine much to my liking. The air is not so soft as it is back in Coroa, but there is something in it that smells of spices, and the beauty and mystery of it all fills me with curiosity each day. It has been good to go away, to be an unknown in a new place. I've made many new acquaintances and have told the great story of you becoming queen to each of them. I daresay you may be the most famous royal of our lifetime.

Speaking of being a famous royal, how are things at home? I remember you mentioning a dozen little ideas before I left. Have any of them come to fruition yet? I remember Hagan being nudged toward you as a suitor. Is he your betrothed now? Did you happen to find someone more to your liking?

It sounds like your reign is off to a very good start, Hollis. Of all people, I know you want to prove yourself. I think you will leave your mark on our country, but only give it time. I think that's what you're doing. I hope so.

All that to say, I have enjoyed studying here in Great Perine, learning about literature, philosophy, and art. I have thought many times that I should make this place my home. I'm not sure I could bear the pitiful or judging eyes of the court in Kereseken Castle again. And yet, the thought of staying away forever makes my chest tighten. Did you feel that way when you went to Isolte? What is it about a home that pulls us back, even when things weren't always good?

Perhaps in the next month or so, I might come back to visit, to see you and your great plans. Maybe then, once I walk through the resplendent halls of Keresken again, I'll know where I'm supposed to be.

I know you are far busier than anyone else on the continent, but once you find time, please do write and tell me of your many adventures. After all this time, you're the one I want to know about the most. I send you my love and my devotion.

Your subject abroad,
Delia Grace

Reading that letter was akin to taking a deep breath. While we had talked through many things before she'd decided to leave, I felt like my life at the castle would never feel quite settled until she was here beside me. By now there was no way that she was the most scandalous one between the two of us, so she wouldn't have to worry about drawing eyes in every room she walked into. But I wondered if there was a part of her that still wished for those eyes to be on her, so long as they didn't find her wanting.

Maybe I'd never know. But I hoped.

I took a deep breath and broke the seal of the last letter.

Your Majesty,
We write to tell you we shall be arriving around nine tomorrow, Thursday the seventeenth. We promise not to make

a scene or tease you. Well, we may tease you, but not too harshly. Not this time.

Etan Rex

I smiled. *Rex.* How fancy. As a fellow sovereign, maybe I would adopt that. But not the royal we, which I intended to taunt him mercilessly about once he arrived. I held the letter up to my nose. I could smell Isolte on the paper, and if I focused, him, too.

He was on his way, and he was still joking with me, and no matter what else was happening, at least there was that.

Never a dull moment, my principal lady came bounding up the pathway.

"Valentina, what is it?"

She was beaming. "It's done, Your Majesty."

I let out a blissful sigh. "Perfect."

THIRTY-SIX

I SAT AT THE VANITY in the king's—well, queen's—chambers as Valentina gave me one last look over. My crown was speckled with sapphires, my ring from Mother shone with its ruby, and my wedding rings? Well, they sat in a safe place so I could see them when I wanted. Jameson and Silas both had their hands on how I'd made it to this place, but the steps I took forward from here all belonged to me. So, I wanted to be perfect today.

Given her past, Valentina was more eagle-eyed than even Delia Grace and was a natural at my side. What's more, we had one another's perfect trust, a thing that had been found and lost and found so many times between Delia Grace and me.

"Valentina, I feel silly for not asking this sooner, but are you uncomfortable being out there today? Not being queen anymore?"

She made a playful face. "Not at all. I'm much happier being your subject than their queen."

"So you don't miss it? Not even being away from Isolte?"

She squinted a moment, thinking. "No. Home is what we make it. And I've made mine here."

"You have been too good to me," I said. "I'll have to find a way to thank you for it someday."

She shook her head, her tone peaceful and resolute. "You rescued me. King Etan rescued me. This is *me* thanking *you*." She stepped back, surveying her handiwork. "There now. Beautiful."

"I wouldn't admit this to anyone else, but I am very nervous."

"With how close you two have been, there's no way this meeting could go poorly."

I swallowed my words, thinking that, with how close we'd been, this could be the hardest meeting of my reign.

Valentina knocked on the door, and the guards opened it for me. I walked through with her tailing my skirt as I serenely acknowledged the crowd. Just beside the dais, Hagan was waiting for me, his arm outstretched.

Hagan was what Valentina had referred to as a "perfect specimen." He was tall with a sharp nose and dark brown hair. His broad shoulders made everything he wore fall impeccably, and, most importantly, he was from one of the oldest families in Coroa. In the days when my mother was trying to parlay what she thought would be a brief relationship with Jameson into a proposal from another high-ranking family, Hagan hadn't even been on her list. He'd been too good for me.

"Good day, Your Majesty," he greeted me, an easy smile on his face. "What an interesting choice. You look lovely."

"Thank you." I practiced breathing steadily as he escorted me in front of the crowd.

My throne was there, as was one for Etan. Hagan had a seat to my right, and on Etan's left, there was another chair for Ayanna. I'd heard he'd been encouraged to find a mate rather quickly. He and I were in similar situations with our family lines: we were the end of them.

I glanced at Valentina, asking her with my eyes if I still looked all right. As if something had changed in the last three minutes. She nodded reassuringly, and I clasped my hands in front of me, hoping to settle my stomach, but instead I felt my ring. I looked down quickly at the gift from Mother, the heirloom from Jedreck. In our many correspondences, Etan had never asked for it, but as I was now a Coroan queen and forbidden from being an Isolten citizen, I wondered if it should go back to him. Just one detail of many to settle over this trip.

The trumpets sounded, announcing their arrival, and I could feel my heart leaping from my chest. Etan was here. We were breathing the same air. I watched expectantly down the path made up the middle of the Great Hall, probably giving away how desperate I was to see his face again.

I saw his shoe first. All it took was a shoe, and I was lost. His hair was shorter, but there was still one rogue piece trying to fall in his eye. He'd grown a very short beard, and it looked absolutely charming around the shape of that smile growing on his face.

I shook my head. I shouldn't have been surprised that we'd had the same thought.

While his entourage was dressed in dozens of cool shades of blue, Etan's coat was red. He was a flash of fire in the night. And I? I'd chosen the bluest gown I had, bedecked my hair in silver. For him.

He walked up, bowing before me. As he did, I noted the petite girl just off his shoulder, her hair done up in an elaborate twist, and her face angelic and poised.

For a split second, I forgot my place. I curtsied to him in return, a little hastily. I sighed. I was already making mistakes.

I walked down off the dais, my arms outstretched, and he happily took my hands in his.

"Is this the best you could do?" he asked, flicking at the collar of my gown. "You look like a puddle."

"I assume they lost your wardrobe on the road and that's why you're wearing this horse blanket?"

He chuckled. "It works in a pinch."

I smiled and looked past him, raising my voice. "Dear friends, thank you for coming. I realize this meeting came much sooner than expected. I appreciate your willingness to visit with us, and for your support, even from afar. Some of you rode up to this very palace for my sake, and I have not forgotten it. Please make yourselves at home. You are most welcome here."

There were courteous claps around the room, and Etan held my hand as we went up the dais. Once we got there, Hagan was waiting for me, and I remembered whose arm I was supposed to be on.

"Your Majesty, please let me introduce you to Sir Hagan Kaltratt. He will be accompanying me for the duration of your stay."

Etan reached out his hand. "A pleasure to meet you, sir. I hope we will get some time to talk ourselves."

Hagan shook Etan's hand in return. "I'd love to. I've heard your quite the jouster. I'd be grateful for any advice you'd be willing to give me."

Etan laughed. "I'm afraid I've only won one tournament. I was lucky." He glanced over to me. "Very lucky. But I'll still go out to the field with you whenever you're free."

"Excellent."

Etan took the hand of the girl beside him, bringing her closer to me. "Your Majesty, I'd like you to meet Lady Ayanna Routhand. She is one of the brightest ladies at the Isolten court, and she's dying for you to give her dancing lessons."

I looked past him. "Is that so?"

She nodded. "I've heard all about your adventures from your mother-in-law. And Lady Scarlet speaks of how you two used to dance."

I grabbed Etan's arm. "Are they here?"

"Held up. They're coming tonight," he replied, an amused smile on his face.

"Your parents?" I had to stop myself from calling them aunt and uncle.

"They're keeping everything together while I'm gone, but they send their love, as always."

I couldn't contain my joy. Etan was here, and Mother would be soon, along with Scarlet. I didn't realize how much I'd been aching for them, but as the moment settled on me, I felt instantly lighter. My standing around and laughing was not the point of the trip, so I motioned for Etan to join me at our seats. Hagan, ever a perfect gentleman, went over to Ayanna, and took her to meet some of the more influential families at court.

"She's sweet," I said.

"Yes. Sweet, eager to learn . . . Father approves, so that's something."

I made a face. "And Aunt Jovana?"

He squinted. "She's a bit more restrained with her affections to Ayanna."

"I'm sure she'll come around."

"I suppose." But there was something about the set of his jaw that said this was unlikely. "What's all this?" he asked pointing to the wall. Next to the stained-glass windows depicting moments from Coroa's past, a curtain hung. "Did a pane get broken?"

"Not broken. I've had a new window installed. We're

unveiling it at sunset. The light should be perfect."

"You would know."

I stared at his smile, lost, completely forgetting where I was supposed to be going or if I was meant to say something. The world was nothing but Etan.

After a moment, he took in a deep breath, like he'd forgotten to inhale. His eyelids fluttered, and he turned to look at the room, seeming to need a distraction almost as much as I did. "You should have seen your people as we approached the first city," he said, his tone balancing perfectly between serious and playful. "Children were waiting by the road with fruit in their hands. They ran alongside us, handing it up to the soldiers and courtiers as we passed."

I beamed with pride. "I've tried to tell you many times; we're generally a welcoming people."

He nodded. "It's hard to believe that on a battlefield. But there were plenty of other times I sh—" He pressed his lips together, his eyes glassy. "Hollis. I said so many things. Terrible things. About you, about Coroa. I called you names. I was so painfully ignorant."

I shook my head. "I cannot judge you; I'm sorry to say I've done the same. But we learn and we change. That's the only way to make anything better."

"Then can you find it in yourself to forgive me?" he whispered.

I stared again, lost in those slate-blue eyes. "For a very long time, there has been nothing to forgive between you and me."

He let out a long, shaky breath, blinking back tears. He

surveyed the people in the Great Hall—both his and mine, Isolten and Coroan—and finding himself pleased with what he saw, he smiled and took me up to the thrones. When we sat his face grew serious.

"How are you faring, Hollis? Tell me the truth."

I swallowed. "Doing well, I think? I have nothing to compare it to. Unlike you, I wasn't born on the edges of royalty, so I've already accidentally broken the law twice just for lack of knowing any better. The holy men held a week-long prayer service for me."

At that, he chuckled. "Well, if anyone could use prayer . . ."

I swatted at him, smiling because, while he was different, he was also just as I remembered him.

"I'm getting better, but I'm terrified of messing something up. It used to be if I made a mistake, it only hurt me, or maybe four or five people around me. Now? I could hurt so many, Etan. It would break my heart."

"Then write me," he said, placing his hand on mine. I thrilled to the touch. "I don't know everything, but I've got plenty of experience. I'll help you."

I tilted my head at him. "You have your own country to tend to. One twice the size of mine, might I add. You can't stop what you're doing to save me."

"But I would," he whispered. "I'd do . . . I'd do so much more if I could."

I swallowed. "I know. Me, too." I lowered my voice. "I can't believe I didn't think about what this would mean . . . for us."

He shrugged. "I didn't, either. In the moment, I was just so pleased for you. To see you become queen."

"If I'd have realized, I never would have . . ."

"Yes, you would have," he insisted. "You'd have taken up your crown in a heartbeat, because, despite my first assessment, you are much more than an ornament. You're brave, possibly to the point of stupidity." I laughed at that. "And you're giving. Unflinchingly loyal . . . so many things, Hollis. Things I wish I'd seen sooner."

I looked away. All the brightness that had surrounded me was fading away. I thought it would be a long-awaited comfort to see Etan again . . . now I wondered how much of it I could take. "I think, for both our sakes, this meeting might need to be the last one in person."

When I dared to lift my gaze to him again, Etan looked as if he might cry. "I think you're right. I don't know if I could do this for the rest of my life."

I nodded. "I'm a little tired. I might excuse myself. But I have so many things I want to ask you about this afternoon, trades to make. I think we can do a lot of good. I will always have a heart for Isolte."

He smiled, a beautiful, defeated thing. "I know. And my heart will always live in Coroa."

I swallowed. I couldn't even say goodbye. I rose and gave him an acceptable curtsy before retreating to my rooms at the fastest pace I could without looking like I'd been offended by something.

I didn't close the door behind me, and Valentina came in

quickly, followed by two of the holy men. They tended to be like shadows for me. Most of the time, I didn't mind it. I was so deeply in need of help, I was thankful anyone came along to usher me in the right direction. I wasn't so sure how I felt about it now.

"Majesty?" Valentina asked, watching as I collapsed into full-on sobs.

"I can't do this," I insisted. "I love him so much, Valentina. How am I supposed to live without him?"

She embraced me. "It's not fair," she agreed. "Too many people have to live without the ones they love. Here you are with every resource in the world, and you still can't make it happen. It's cruel, Hollis. I'm sorry."

"Majesty?" Langston asked. "He did not offend you, did he?"

I shook my head, weeping. How could I explain what everyone in close quarters already knew: my heartache was my own doing.

I clutched Valentina. I felt so foolish, picking up the crown and taking vows before I'd known it meant Etan would be gone forever, before I realized being sovereigns meant that Etan and I were tied to our own countries with no means of escape.

The holy men weren't sure what to do with a crying woman. They'd said the wrong thing to me more than once, and now they usually chose to stay silent in the absence of the right words.

"Majesty," Langston said, "for what it's worth, we are

sorry. When you left, we thought we knew what heartbreak looked like. Jameson was all but inconsolable. Still, we never saw him break. He was angry, vain, vengeful . . . it was never like this with him." He came closer to me, speaking softly. "But we know your strength. And your people love you. You will overcome this."

I nodded my head and spoke through my tears. "Of course, I will. My apologies. I will rest and be ready for our meeting this afternoon. We have much work to do on this trip, and I will not let you down."

The holy men bowed and backed out of the room, closing the door behind them.

"Come," Valentina said. "Let's get all the tears out now. It won't do for everyone to see them."

"If anyone understands that, it's you."

She held me tighter. "I do. And I won't let you fall, Hollis."

The sad thing was, I'd already fallen. And I was in so deep there was no coming back.

THIRTY-SEVEN

"I'M AFRAID I HAVE A rather long list," I warned Etan as I walked around the wide table in my new offices. The holy men were standing at their own desk, books and scrolls on hand should anything need confirmation. Ayanna and Hagan sat side by side in chairs, whispering questions and answers to one another, the intendeds of two young sovereigns.

"I do, too," he said, setting some papers on the large table in front of us. "Ladies first."

I smiled. "Well, even before I was queen, I envied Isolte's medical advances. I would like to start some sort of program where Coroan citizens who have an interest in medicine could study in Isolte. Of course, it would be limited, and people would need to apply; I don't want to send a hoard your way. But would you be agreeable to something like that?"

He considered. "Why don't I send some of our brightest here? Perhaps we could do rotating courses. Maybe go to two or three regions in Coroa? You'd know where they'd be most useful."

I blinked. "That would be incredibly generous. Off the top of my head, I'd want something here, where the population is so dense and in need of care, and something in the poorest areas where getting care is the most difficult. Once a handful of people were trained, they could take over the teaching roles, and your doctors could go home."

He nodded. "Note that we need to make inquiries for ten doctors willing to come and teach in Coroa. Housing and payment will be taken care of."

One of his pages wrote this down.

"Thank you," I breathed, standing a little bit taller. "That was easy. All right. Your turn. What do you want the most?"

He turned and looked at me for a long time. It wasn't the best choice of words, a question neither of us could honestly answer. I heard Hagan clear his throat, and I finally moved away.

Etan reached for a scroll. "This is the project I'm fondest of." He rolled the paper out, placing two weights on the edges so I could see the outline of a map of the continent.

I squinted, letting my fingers wader around the map. "I don't think I understand."

He pointed at a faint red line along where Coroa and Isolte met. "When you told Quinten he should simply give the land over, it was one of the best ideas I'd ever heard.

With the turnover of sovereigns recently," he began, giving me a pointed look, "I haven't heard of any skirmishes along the border. It seems people are otherwise occupied. But before there's a chance for animosities to build up again, I want to cut it down. I suggest a new border, giving these two sections of land to Coroa." He traced along the red line, and I could see now how it dipped ever so slightly into Isolte, barely taking anything from the mass overall, but changing everything.

I leaned close to Etan, whispering. "I can't help but notice that so far, everything is of a benefit to me."

"It's all I can do, Hollis. Please don't stop me."

I swallowed. This time it was Ayanna who cleared her throat.

I tried to hide it, tried to not look as if my world revolved around his smile. I felt positive every inch of my face gave me away, and try as I may, there was nothing I could do about it. I peeked over my shoulder at Etan's intended. I had the distinct feeling both she and Hagan would be thrilled when this trip was over.

"Very well. Granted," I said quietly.

"Oh, amazing. You've learned to take instruction. I can't wait to write Mother about this."

"Writing? So you've finally mastered the alphabet, then? She must be so proud."

Talks over trade and roads and art went on for hours, and, for the life of me, I didn't understand why the people before us made things so difficult. While Etan and I didn't see perfectly eye to eye on everything, and while those who kept the laws had to interject from time to time, everything went smoothly.

Going into these talks assuming my neighboring king wasn't trying to ruin me and knowing this queen wasn't trying to ruin him changed everything.

Worlds could be changed when we chose not to walk into rooms operating as if everyone was our enemy.

Etan finally rubbed at his forehead. "I think I have to stop for now. We can leave all the papers out and pick up here tomorrow if you like."

I nodded. "And I think they've planned a ball tonight, so I need rest before that."

"Well, you don't have to dance, Your Majesty," Hagan offered. "I'm sure the other ladies of court will be happy to entertain our guests in your stead."

Ayanna stood. "Some of the ladies from Isolte choreographed a piece for you. A gift. Nothing impressive, I'm sure, but—"

"No, no!" I said, smiling. "How thoughtful. I can't wait to see." I turned to Etan.

"Completely her idea," he bragged. I liked that she was considerate. He needed someone who put him first, others first in general.

"Gentlemen, will you excuse us? I think I'd like to show Lady Ayanna the gardens."

She smiled as her eyes went wide, and she let out a slow breath as if bracing herself for being alone in my company.

"Come," I said, giving her my arm. "You're going to love the flowers."

We made our way outside, and, as we walked, I pointed out the fine features of our architecture and noted the various wings of the castle. My home.

For so long, I'd felt like I wasn't sure where that was. But this was my home now. Right? It had to be. It was where I slept, where I ate, where I ruled. But I supposed that, as long as Etan Northcott wasn't under the same roof, no place would ever feel like home to me.

"So, what did you want to talk about?" Ayanna ventured. "I'm sure you didn't bring me out here just to look at flowers."

"Well, I thought it would be nice to get to know you. I'm sure we'll correspond over the years, even if we don't meet again."

"Is . . . are you planning not to meet again?"

"It's unlikely." I ignored her shaky breath of relief. "But tell me about yourself. How did you meet Etan?"

She smiled, thinking back. "My parents introduced us. I was sick for Hadrian's wedding, so I missed meeting you, watching His Majesty win the tournament, and seeing him come back with an army. After everything was settled and I was well again, we went to Chetwin to pay tribute and pledge our loyalty. I've been at the castle ever since, so we get to spend a lot of time together." She added a shy little shrug. "How did you meet His Majesty?"

I giggled. "Oh, it was here in the Great Hall. He insulted

me, and I gave it right back. We were off to a fantastic start."

She laughed. "Really? I've never heard Etan insult anyone."

I rolled my eyes. "Lucky you. It seems we communicate in irritating one another."

Ayanna stopped, dropping my arm. "Then how is it . . . why do you seem so happy when you're in the same room?"

I was confident I was blushing, but I still went to deny it. "He's like family. I married his—"

She cut me off. "No, I know the whole story. But he's been smiling to himself for a week. And in that room, he'd reach for something just to touch your hand. So, if you two live to argue with each other, why does it seem like . . ." She couldn't bring herself to finish. "I'm strong enough to take it, you know. I can resolve myself to losing him; I just need someone to tell me the truth."

So here it was, one of many moments I'd been dreading. I wanted to tell her to stop fighting for him, that if it came down to it, I'd win every time. But I couldn't. I couldn't fight for Etan or waste my time hating her.

Ayanna was the only one who could take care of him in my place, so my sole choice was to be honest and to love her through it. I had to be her champion.

I took her by both arms. "The truth is, he means the world to me. I won't be so cruel as to lie to you. But he has to come in second place to Coroa. I took *vows* to serve Coroa, and I cannot leave my throne. Much like Etan, there's no one left to take it. So, you needn't fear. I am here, and he is there, and after this trip, you will most likely never see my face again."

She looked down and then out to the garden. The blooms were still hanging on, but fall was upon us. Soon, everything here would go to sleep.

"You say Etan will always come in second place to Coroa. But I will always come in second place to you," she lamented.

"No," I insisted. "We went through something monumental together. It forged a friendship deeper than most. But we will part ways, and he will marry you. Over time, things will be different, I promise."

This was not the conversation I'd imagined us having. I simply wanted to know her character better. But I knew my role in this world, and it painted me into one corner and Etan into another. If all I could leave him with was a confident bride-to-be, then that was what I'd do.

"What about Hagan?" she asked. "He seems incredibly kind."

I laced my arm back through hers and kept us moving. Maybe if we just kept walking, things would somehow resolve themselves.

"He is. He's perfect, really. Handsome, considerate, always thinks of me first. I can't imagine another man in Coroa doing a better job as my consort." I made a point of wording that carefully, and I wondered if she caught it. "Hagan will be my prince, you will be Etan's queen, and I'd like to think that we could be friends."

Her head tilted over, looking to me. "Really?"

I nodded. "Truly."

She smiled, a cautious and fragile thing. She wasn't a terrible girl. In some ways, things would have been so much easier if she had been.

"Have you ever made a flower crown?" I asked her. "Come, we'll have to make you one for tonight."

THIRTY-EIGHT

THANKS TO SILAS, I'D LEARNED many things. I'd learned what love looked like. I'd learned that playfulness and seriousness could walk hand in hand. And, most practically, I'd learned that lots of things could be done with metal.

"This is quite pretty," Nora commented. "Where in the world did you get a golden feather?"

I smiled at my reflection. "Oh, somewhere along the way."

With the spaces left between the barbs, it was easy for my seamstress to weave golden thread through them and attach it to the front of my gown, all blindingly bright and beautiful. Someone might say it was ostentatious to have something so large laced into the bodice of my gown, but if I couldn't come out and tell Etan how desperately I missed him, then I'd show him that he was directly by my heart at all times by whatever means I had.

I'd gone back to my traditional gold. I wasn't sure, but I thought he liked me in gold. And though it was proper to wear my crown, I laced flowers from the garden into it, so I could try to be Hollis and queen at the same time. Tonight would be slightly less formal, and I wanted to leave him with images of me that he could hold close, no matter what came our way. And many things certainly would. Two different countries, two inevitable weddings, and years of ruling side by side but hardly ever speaking.

We'd survived so much already. We could survive this.

When I walked into the Great Hall, dinner was already in progress.

Two men from Isolte came up to me, bowing down to one knee. "Your Majesty, I don't know if you would remember us, but we served King Etan when you came to confront Jameson. We know you played a huge role in finally bringing us a just king, and we are glad to see Coroa now has a fair queen. We wanted to pay our respects."

They lowered their heads, showing more humility than I thought I deserved. "Gentlemen, you risked your lives more than once that day. It is I who should be honoring you."

"Oh, no, miss," one replied adamantly. "We've heard all about your bravery. His Majesty speaks so highly of you."

I laughed. "Well, I know how hard it is to win his praise, so I will take that as the greatest of compliments. Please rise, sirs, and enjoy yourselves. I hope you're feeling most welcome."

They both came up, a strange expression on their faces.

The one who'd been silent gestured haphazardly around the room. "I've been to Coroa countless times, and I've never felt so at home. I have to attribute it to having a fair and generous queen," he said.

"Thank you, sir. That means a lot to me."

They both nodded again and went to join the festivities.

Hagan found me as they left and walked around two steps behind me like a duckling. I found myself pausing to study him.

He was everything I told Ayanna. Attentive, handsome. And he would be a good father, I could see that. He had no great ambitions and didn't ask for anything. From what I could tell, he didn't seem bothered by the idea of having a wife who outranked him . . . he was as good as I could hope for.

"Look how well things are going, Your Majesty," he said, gazing out upon the room. I followed his eyes, and he was right.

The last time the people of Coroa and Isolte met in this castle, there had been petty fighting and an air of mistrust over the entire trip. I saw those in blue toasting with those in red, people with dark hair clapping those with stark blonde on the back when they made a joke. It was so very . . . happy.

I was so wrapped up in my thoughts that I barely registered that someone had stopped in front of me.

"Your Majesty."

I turned to the figure bent down but looking directly at me and started crying without a second thought.

"Mother!" I yanked her up and fell into her arms. Oh, I'd needed this. I needed someone to hold me and care for me in a way that no one else could. I needed someone who loved me.

"My turn." I looked up to see Scarlet waiting behind her and I moved directly from one hug to the other. "I've missed you so much."

"Not as much as I've missed you."

They held on to me, there in the middle of the Great Hall, and for the first time in weeks, I felt whole. I knew they'd go back to Isolte, that I couldn't keep them. But, for today, I had a family.

"Sorry we're late," Scarlet said. "His Majesty has given us duties at court, and there was a little hiccup. He's been so good to us, we don't want to let him down."

Just over her shoulder, Julien gave me a polite nod, beaming as he looked around the room. I was thrilled to see he was still by Scarlet's side.

I took her hand. "How is Etan doing? Tell me what you know he wouldn't."

Scarlet smiled. She really smiled. The girl who danced in my chambers had come back after all this time. "He's doing so well, Your Majesty. You have nothing to worry about. He's weeding out those who served in the Darkest Knights, and he's been cleaning the city near the castle. Every day, he has a new idea of how to make Isolte better. People have embraced him with open arms, and we are a peaceful country. At last."

The tension fell out of my shoulders. "Thank goodness. Then I have all I could ask for."

Almost.

"Pardon me."

It sent a thrill up my spine that I knew his voice under any circumstance. I turned and Etan was there.

"If I might steal you from your family, I think you and I should set the example, Your Majesty." He held out his hand.

Beside him, Ayanna smiled, tilting her head, telling me this was fine. I looked back to Hagan.

He raised his hands in the air and spoke with an easy smile. "Who am I to contradict a king?"

"Very well," I said, sighing.

As he led me out to the center of the room, the couples on the floor cleared for us. When we were standing face-to-face, I watched as his intent eye went over my face, doing what I knew I was doing, and putting every detail to memory.

Finally, his eyes fell on my dress. "I always wondered what happened to that feather. It makes you look like a warrior. I rather like it."

The music started, and the familiar notes of the song we'd danced to once before filled the room. Of course. We bowed and curtsied and stepped around each other. "I like to think it gives us a little luck."

We moved to face each other again. "I keep our luck with me, too," he said, reaching up to double tap the pocket on his coat. The golden fringe of a familiar handkerchief hung out of it.

I spun, keeping my eyes on his pocket. "I thought you said you lost it."

He shook his head. "I never lost it. I just didn't want to give it back." Then, thinking better of it, he spoke again. "Well, I lost it once, and I tore my room apart looking for it. I don't go anywhere without it in my pocket."

"When did you become such a romantic?" I teased.

"I always was. You just hated me too much to see it."

I playfully pursed my lips in thought. "I only really hated you for a day. Maybe."

"I wish I could say the same," he said, shaking his head. "If I'd known how limited our time was, how much it would matter, I wouldn't have wasted it."

"We have one more day. Let's not make the same mistake."

He nodded silently as we continued moving. Why had this dance felt so much longer in Isolte? The song was coming to a close, and he was going to lift me. This might be the last excuse I ever had in my life to be held by Etan.

He swept me into the air, eyes locked on mine . . . and he never brought me down. He just held me up, looking into my eyes, until the music stopped.

When he finally brought me down, the room was applauding our dance, and I was a little breathless.

A sea of eyes, and I could only see his. I felt myself leaning into him, closer and closer. He swallowed before looking away, and I found myself very much in need of a distraction.

"I suppose now's as good a time as any. Here." I took his

hand and pulled him over to the side of the room with the windows. I nodded to Hagan and Ayanna, who were talking with their heads together. I wondered what secrets they were sharing. Whatever it was, they dropped them to join us. Some of the holy men were already there, being attentive as always.

"Langston, would you reveal the window, so I might show our guest."

Though he had expressed his concerns over the new window at first, Langston couldn't argue that our moment in history was unprecedented. He nodded to another man, who very enthusiastically reached over and pulled the drape. The sun was still a little high, but it lit the window perfectly. I watched Etan's face as he took in the scene.

"That's you," he breathed.

I nodded. Yes, it was me. I was emblazoned in a red dress with my hair out behind me, standing just outside the castle. But the window was not simply a tribute to myself. In the background was the outline of dozens of men in blue, and just in front of them . . .

"And that's me!"

I lowered my voice. "I will see you every day. And all the people of Coroa will know who you are, what you did for us."

I watched his Adam's apple travel up and down as he tried to keep his tears in check.

"This is too much, Hollis."

"It's all I can do. Nothing feels like quite enough."

He was swallowing hard. "I love it. I love . . ." He looked down at me, never finishing his sentence.

We were trapped by our crowns, and it was an excruciating kind of pain to know just how much we loved each other and to be completely unable to do anything about it.

"If you'll excuse me, Your Majesty. I think the excitement of the day has made me tired." He turned so that his fingers gently brushed against mine and went from the room. Ayanna followed, and I couldn't quite read her face. Was she sad? Disappointed? Whatever it was, it didn't seem good. In her wake, Mother and Scarlet came up.

"That's a beautiful gesture, Your Majesty," Mother said.

"Can I please just be Hollis to you?" I asked, very near tears.

Scarlet wrapped her arms around my waist as Mother affectionately ran her hand over my hair. "Of course. You will always be my Hollis. But look at what you've become! And look what you've accomplished. Etan was fighting with everyone and everything; he'd given up on his life, and you saved it. And you! You confronted the monsters in your life and set horrific wrongs to right. You're the first queen regnant in Coroa's history, and, my goodness, just look around this room."

I did. I really took it in.

"You have joined what most people thought never could be. That alone is an accomplishment for the history books," she said.

Something struck me just then. Something stupid and reckless and maybe impossible. But I had nothing else to lose, so I was certainly going to try.

"Get Valentina. And Nora, too. I need you all. I need your help."

THIRTY-NINE

THE SUN WAS STREAMING THROUGH the windows, and I was still reading over the law. Mother, Scarlet, Valentina, Nora, and I traded the books to one another repeatedly, checking everything between the five of us.

Valentina let out a gaping yawn. "I don't think it's *illegal*. I just can't be sure no one could argue your position. Nora?"

"The language they use is impossible. I keep needing to use the dictionary. Why don't they write this out plainly?" she moaned.

Scarlet wiped at her eyes. "I didn't see anything against it. But, you know, things started blurring together about four hours ago."

"I think I may pass out," Mother added.

"I know, I'm so sorry," I apologized drowsily. "But

everyone's leaving this evening, so if I'm going to do something, I have to do it now."

Exhausted but faithful, my friends and family turned back to the law books and history books strewn out before us. I felt like I was shooting arrows in the dark, trying to find something I wasn't sure existed.

"Hollis . . ." Valentina's eyes were suddenly sharper, and I watched as she read over a section of the law again. "Look at this."

She handed one of the large books to me, pointing to a passage. I read it three times to make sure I'd gotten it right. "I think this is it . . . Valentina, I think you found it!"

"Oh, thank goodness," Scarlet sighed. "Can I sleep now?"

"My bed is that way," I offered. "All of you, get some rest. I'll get someone else to dress me, Valentina. You've already done too much."

She shook her head. "If you're doing this, I can't trust it to anyone else. Come on."

I followed her to my room, where Mother and Scarlet unceremoniously fell into my bed. Nora, the sweet thing, fell awkwardly into a very large chair, and was out in seconds. I thought of the most recent sleepless nights in my life. One where we walked to Varinger Hall. One where Etan chased me as I ran for the border. One where I cried reading his letter explaining our situation. And then last night.

I refused to count any of those nights as wasted, but this one left me feeling so very hopeful.

Valentina laced me into another something red. So much of my wardrobe was red. I splashed water on my face, and she pulled my hair up, so it looked presentable. I stared at myself in the mirror, trying to steady my resolve.

"What's step one?" Valentina asked.

"Hagan."

She nodded. "Makes sense. How does it look?"

I surveyed everything she'd done. "Perfect. As always. Thank you."

"Do you want me to come with you?"

I laughed at her drooping eyes. "No. I think I have to do this alone."

"Oh, thank goodness," she said, flopping onto a nearby couch.

I left her, moving swiftly through the still-quiet castle. There was a good chance that Hagan was still in bed, and I was about to give him the rudest awakening of his life. People bowed as I passed, making my way to his room. Once there, I stood, telling myself with each new breath I was going to knock. It took several minutes for me to finally do it.

His butler opened the door, and once he saw me, he fell into a bow, looking very nervous.

"Laurence, could you please tell Sir Hagan that I am here. I will wait for him to dress if he needs."

Laurence stood, handing a folded letter to me. "That won't be necessary, Your Majesty."

I took the note and cracked the seal, taking in a quickly scribbled letter.

Hollis,

I'm sorry. I know you want love, and so do I, and it doesn't look like we'll find that with each other. I'm so, so sorry. A better man might have been able to do it. I hope you find someone who can stand in the place where I cannot.

Hagan

Perhaps my first reaction shouldn't have been relief.

"Did he say where he was going?"

"No, Your Majesty."

I stood there for a moment, stunned. Not angry, just . . . surprised.

"If you learn, please let me know, so I might send my blessing. Thank you."

I turned away, trying to think. I supposed it stung a little to find that even a crown couldn't make life with me tolerable to Hagan. Then again, the same was true of me and Jameson. No, I wouldn't hold this against him. Someday, I'd find a way to thank him. Really, that's what he deserved.

With that done, the only thing to do now was go to Etan. I kept imagining his rejection. If nothing else, he was devoted to Isolte, and his character was so strong that he'd be loath to hurt Ayanna. This could end quite badly indeed.

I swallowed and went up the stairway to his room. I did

the same ridiculous dance in my head, saying I just needed to breathe a little more first. But in the middle of my useless ritual, I heard talking behind the door.

I knocked and was greeted by Etan himself. He was holding a piece of paper in his hands, looking perplexed. After he flung the door wide, he went back to using that free hand to tuck in his shirt and straighten his doublet. His hair was a wild mess, but it suited him.

"Hollis, do you know anything about this?" he asked, holding up the paper.

"What is it?"

"It was slipped under my door last night. Ayanna's gone."

I felt the blood drain from my face. I sighed. "I might know something. Can you . . . can we have your staff leave for a moment?"

Still looking like he was asked to solve a riddle before he could pass a bridge, he nodded, staring into nothing. The butlers and dressers left, closing the door behind them.

"This is my fault," he said. "I should have been more attentive to her. I got swept up in needing to give you the best goodbye that I could, and I don't think she could see past it. I brought this on myself."

"She . . . we talked. She knew there was a light at the end of the tunnel, and she was hopeful. You did nothing."

He looked over at me, shocked. "You talked?"

"Yes. Women do that. I highly recommend it. Solves so many problems."

"Didn't solve this one," he said bitterly, throwing himself into a chair.

"We spoke yesterday afternoon," I told him. "Something must have happened between then and now. My best guess is that she and Hagan bonded over their positions in our lives."

He looked up at me through the fingers that were propping up his head. "What makes you say that?"

"Oh, nothing. Just that he's gone, too." I held up my letter.

Etan hopped up. "Do you think they left together?"

"How would an Isolten girl know where to run unless a Coroan boy took her?"

His shoulders slumped and he started pacing. "Hollis . . . I'm so sorry. Messing up my life is its own thing, but yours?"

"I'm used to it," I said with a shrug.

Despite his disappointed mood, he laughed. "How are you so calm about this? You and I both have to marry *someone*. We have to establish lines, and the most fitting options for either of us are gone."

I shook my head, smiling. Tears came to my eyes as I whispered, "No, Etan. No, they're not."

He stopped walking and stared at me, looking equal parts hopeful and nervous. We probably matched in that sense.

"Hollis?" he asked, his eyes still hesitant.

I cleared my throat. "Do you remember how you suggested a new border between Isolte and Coroa?"

"Yes. I still mean it. It's the thing I'm most passionate about."

"Well, what if we just . . . eliminated the border?"

His forehead folded in confusion. "What?"

"What if Isolte gave Coroa all its land? And what if Coroa gave Isolte all *its* land? And what if . . . what if there was no border between you and me?"

His face softened. "No border?"

"No border."

"One country?"

"One country."

I saw all the wheels in his head spring to life. "So, instead of two thrones in two castles in two countries . . . those thrones would be in one country, one castle?"

"With a circular throne room," I proposed.

"And a garden maze. Obviously," he added.

"Valentina, Nora, Mother, Scarlet, and I stayed up all night reading the law, dissecting everything. We would need to word it differently, but it is well within my rights and power as queen to acquire new land, to absorb other countries into ours. Seeing as Isolte is also a land of laws, I'm sure you have similar powers. We can find a way around one law with another. We could be together." I looked at him and shrugged. "What do you think?"

He charged at me, crashing his lips against mine. I held on to him, dying to have him closer. There was simply too much air.

"Could we make this work?" he asked genuinely. "They're still two different peoples."

"Not like they used to be, Etan. I've been watching so

carefully over this trip. Things have changed. Probably because of us. It is surprisingly easy to teach people not to hate. I think it will work, Etan. I really do."

He looked me up and down. "We'll have to start wearing purple."

"That'll work. I look good in everything."

"Eh, I suppose," he teased, gripping me tighter, and kissing me again.